COURAGE STOLEN

A NOVEL

BY
R. SCOTT MACKEY

Big Hound Publishing
Sacramento, CA

Get a FREE Copy of Courage Begins

Read the first book in the Ray Courage series

(Go to http://www.rscottmackey.com/?page_id=163
for free download page)

In this novella, Ray Courage begins his private investigation career,
displaying the skills, abilities and sense of humor that have made him a
fan favorite around the world.

Also by R. Scott Mackey

In the Ray Courage Mystery Series

COURAGE RESURRECTED
COURAGE MATTERS
COURAGE BEGINS (A NOVELLA)

For updates, giveaways, and discounts, join Scott's reader list:
http://www.rscottmackey.com/?page_id=163

For Carney and Dace

one

JERRY LANGFORD, GRANDERSON UNIVERSITY'S chief of security, knew his was the most difficult and important job in California, or pretty much anywhere this side of Washington, DC. That's about all I'd gleaned during the first thirty minutes of our meeting in his basement office. I wanted to ask him the significance of the security chief being located where he would never see the light of day but refrained from doing so because Langford had yet to exhibit anything resembling a sense of humor.

"We may be a small school, at last count about twenty-four hundred undergraduate and graduate students, but the work here is cutting edge, top notch." He was sitting back in his chair, fingertips steepled below his chin. I thought he might hoist his feet onto his desk, but this was one affectation he avoided. The small office was lit with a single desktop halogen lamp the size of a pencil eraser pointed at the ceiling. Behind him, I counted a dozen security monitors fed by cameras positioned throughout the campus. There were video images of building exteriors, interior hallways, classrooms, and labs. He glanced every now and then to check the screens.

"Impressive system," I said, pointing at the monitors.

"State of the art. Twenty-four seven, video and audio."

I nodded. "Why do you like it so dark in here?"

"Is it? I hadn't noticed."

"Like a cave."

1

"Well, I suppose I've grown used to it. Anyway, as I was saying—
"

"You mentioned last night on the phone something about a theft or a sabotaged project." I couldn't take another thirty minutes on the theory of university law enforcement. If he couldn't find a point, I'd damn well lead him to it.

"Yes, I was getting to that Mr. Courage, or is it Dr. Courage?"

"Ray is fine. You can make the check out anyway you want. But please go on about the reason you called me."

He reached across his desk and picked up a small spiral notebook, flipped through a few pages, and read for several seconds before explaining the reason for our meeting. "Last night about seven, I received a near hysterical call from a PhD student over at Frankenstein's lab. She said someone had stolen their drawings for a prototype and had destroyed all their data on some micro-something genome research."

"You have a Frankenstein lab?"

"No, no, no. That's just what everyone calls it. Everything there is secretive. No one knows what goes on in there, except for Professor Wiggin, who runs the place, and his doctoral students."

"Not even the chief of security?"

If he recognized my jab, he chose to ignore it. "I'm much too busy to know the details of every research project on this campus."

"Of course you are."

"Are you messing with me, Ray?"

"Wouldn't think of it."

He gave me about five seconds of a well-practiced cop stare down. I gave him my well-practiced impish grin.

"How did you hear about me?" I asked. He'd been vague on the phone.

"Nick Trujillo recommended you."

"*Lieutenant* Nick Trujillo?"

Langford nodded. Trujillo had arrested me for murder a year earlier, and as far as I could tell, hated my guts. Even after the charges were dropped, he looked at me like I'd tried to sell him dirty pictures of his kids.

"He said you were a good investigator. Discreet. And because you used to work at a university you might know your way around here. You look surprised."

"Just didn't realize Lieutenant Trujillo held me in such high regard."

"No matter. I think we had better move this discussion along. It's taking far too long," he said, as if it was my fault he'd spent the first forty minutes bloviating about himself.

"So there's a theft or sabotage of—"

"*Alleged* theft or *alleged* sabotage."

"Okay, fine. But why are you hiring me and not investigating it yourself?"

He laughed. Apparently, he had a sense of humor after all. "I don't have the resources. In addition to myself, I have two sworn officers. I'm supposed to be getting four more, but that doesn't seem to be a priority for the university president or board of trustees."

"Your police force is three people? I don't mean to sound rude, but you made it sound earlier that you were academia's version of the palace guards."

"You can infer whatever you want into my previous comments." His eyes narrowed, face reddening. "But the fact is, I don't have the time to investigate this claim. And, quite frankly, my two officers lack the training to do so."

"Why not call the city police?"

"Because no matter what did or didn't happen over in that lab, it could turn into a public relations nightmare for the university if word got out we had to call the police. We do not want any negative publicity. As you know, we are only fifteen years old. We've had remarkable growth, remarkable success. We are starting to be seen nationally as a top-tier university, a place—"

"You told me that already, somewhere right after ethical responsibility and educational freedom." It was rude. I didn't care.

"Are you going to keep interrupting me?" His eyes bore into me, and I thought he might fire me before I even started.

"Go on."

"Fine. As I was saying, if it gets out that this institution's academic integrity is less than stellar, our reputation—our hard-earned reputation—will be shot down in flames."

"So you hired me to keep things under the radar."

"Yes, and I'm beginning to regret it."

"No need to worry about a thing. I'm all over this."

A few minutes later, I left Langford's office and walked across the Granderson campus towards the Sieboldt Science Center, home to the so-called Frankenstein lab. I stopped to sit on a bench and review the file Langford had given me before sending me on my way. It was a cold February day, and rain clouds darkened the mid-morning sky. The campus occupied Rosetown's eastern edge, which at an elevation of three thousand feet received an occasional dusting of snow.

The campus was small, about the size of an urban high school, its building tending more towards high tech with lots of glass and steel rather than traditional red brick and archways. Scores of students strolled from one building to another, apparently making their way from one class to another. They were a comely lot, hair in place, clothes tidy, their straight teeth the marvel of modern orthodontics. Quite a contrast to the mixed bag of students I taught during my tenure as a communications professor at Sacramento State University, where students balanced minimum wage jobs, student loans, and overcrowded classrooms in pursuit of a public school degree. I wondered if the forty-two thousand dollar tuition Granderson charged got you more than a Sac State degree other than free and abundant parking and the chance to marry a fellow blueblood.

I flipped open the folder and read the first page. It was the curriculum vitae for Professor Kenneth Wiggin printed from a webpage.

> *Degrees:*
>
> *1972—Doctoral Fellow, Harvard University, Molecular and Cellular Biology*
>
> *1967—PhD, University of California, San Francisco, Genetics*
>
> *1961—BA, University of Colorado, Cellular and Developmental Biology*
>
> *Research Interests:*
>
> *My focus is on the discovery of microbial organisms for purposes of genome sequencing and gaining insight for developing energy-related biotechnologies such as photosynthetic systems and organisms that can metabolize available renewable resources and waste material. Given that less than 0.01% of all microbes have been cultivated, this research field holds significant potential for academic insight and commercial advances in energy supply.*

The vitae went on to list his publications, memberships, and other activities of interest to other academics. It was a lot of blah, blah, blah that didn't shed much insight into what they were doing in his lab. The second paper in the folder was more of a brief bio:

> *PhD candidate Candace Symington holds a bachelor's degree in genetics from Stanford University and master's degrees in both mathematics and biology from Cornell. She has published fifteen different papers on micro-*

bial genomics, including her full genomic characterizations of eight unique bacteria and three protozoa. Ms. Symington is working with Dr. Kenneth Wiggin on commercial applications for microbial sequencing.

I still didn't have much of a clue about what went on in Wiggin's lab, but the word "commercial" popped twice. Closing the file, I stood and headed towards the science center.

two

According to the small sign outside the door, Candace Symington shared an office with someone named Jack Cassidy. A few seconds after I knocked on the closed door, a twenty-something woman opened it.

"Yes?" She showed no expression as her eyes surveyed me.

"Candace Symington?"

"Yes. And you are?

"Ray Courage. The head of Granderson's security said something might have happened to a project you're working on. He asked me to follow up with you."

Her chin dropped to her chest, and I thought she might cry. "Yes," she said, just above a whisper.

"Do you have a few minutes to talk about it?"

"I was going to get some coffee. Okay if we talk at the student café?"

Her hands shook as she locked the office door, and she accidentally dropped the foam keychain loaded with several keys. The Granderson University seal, printed in royal blue on one side, was beginning to rub off. I bent over and picked the keys up for her.

"Thanks. I guess I'm a bit unnerved by this whole thing, especially since I got this note this morning."

"A note?"

"I'll show it to you when get to the café."

We walked down the stairs and outside. She was an attractive young woman, medium height and build, with light brown hair and the bangs that had become the style on college campuses. Her face was pretty: soft brown eyes and firm cheekbones accented with a hint of blush. She wore Top-Sider flats, expensive jeans, and a simple green top over which she had thrown a black wool coat. She led us to the café three buildings from her office.

"Are you a policeman?"

"No, private investigator."

"Really? I didn't know there really were private investigators. I thought they were just on television."

"Here I am."

Inside, she selected a bran muffin and poured herself a tall cup of coffee. I settled for just coffee. After paying the cashier, we settled in at a corner table next to a picture window. Through the windows of the building next door, I could see several students running on treadmills while others hoisted dumbbells or battled the weight machines.

"I'm glad to see Chief Langford took me seriously." She peeled the paper from the base of her muffin. "Though, I was hoping he was going to call the police. No offense."

"None taken. He still might. He just wanted me to do a preliminary investigation, I guess you could say."

"You mean he wants you to see if I'm full of crap or if what I said happened actually did."

"There's that."

"Thank you for not bullshitting me at least."

I took a sip of my coffee. "Do you mind telling me what happened?"

She sighed. "I guess the short version is someone stole Project Monarch. Three long, hard years of work."

"What's Professor Wiggin say about the whole thing?"

"I haven't heard from him yet. He's in Germany. I e-mailed him last night."

"Tell me what's missing and when you discovered it was gone."

"It was about six o'clock last night. Jack and I had been working in the lab pretty much all day and—"

"Jack Cassidy?" I remembered the name from the sign by her office door.

"Yes. He's also a PhD candidate. In biofuels engineering. Brilliant guy. So we knocked off sometime after five o'clock. We left the lab at the same time. I was about halfway home—I live a couple miles away here in Rosetown—when something came to me about a problem I was having on the project. A little detail I hadn't been able to work through. You know how it is, your subconscious mind solves problems when you aren't even thinking about it."

I nodded and took another sip of coffee.

"So, when I get back to the lab and fire up my laptop, I can't find it."

"Can't find what?"

"Anything—the prototype designs, three years of lab test results, any of the related microbial genome sequences. Everything on the computer was gone. Three years' work all gone."

"Did your hard drive crash or something?"

"No, no. The hard drive was fine. All my other files were untouched. Just the project was taken or deleted or whatever."

"You have backup files, right?"

"Of course. I called Jack, and he came back so we could check his laptop. Same thing. All the data was erased from his computer, too. I mean, less than an hour earlier it was all there. We were both working on it, had saved everything, and then uploaded it to our server."

"It's on the server then? It's just not on your laptops?"

"I wish. The server was stolen. We have a dedicated server located away from the lab for security reasons. Great security, huh?"

"Wait a minute, when did you find out the server was missing?"

"Not long after Jack and I realized what had happened to our laptops. We tried to connect to the server from our laptops but kept getting a 'drive not configured' message. That's never happened before. I mean, we had backed everything up less than an hour earlier. It was standard protocol. We backed up to the server twice each day—before lunch and at the end of the work day."

She paused and picked at her muffin, tore off a piece no bigger than her thumbnail, nibbled at it, and then washed it down with a sip of coffee.

"Did you try to reconfigure your connection to the server?"

"Didn't work." She shook her head as she tore off another small piece of muffin. "We were panicked, so we went over to the administration building where the university server farm is and demanded to see—to physically see—our server. We'd never been there before, never seen the damn thing. Even the tech guy couldn't tell us straight off which one was ours. I mean, there's something like fifty or sixty servers over there. He checks his records and takes us to the rack where our server is supposed to be. And, of course, it's gone. Big empty space where the fucking thing is supposed to be."

"Wait a second. If you had backed everything up at about five, and by now it's about six or so, wouldn't the tech support employee have seen someone steal the server?"

She shook her head. "He had come here to the café for his dinner break. He said he locked the door to the server farm area, but who knows?"

"Security camera?"

She shook her head. "Supposedly it's on the to-do list, but as of now, there's no camera on the server farm or the entrance to it. At least that's what the IT guy said."

"Does Jerry Langford know about the theft of the server?"

"I don't know. Maybe. IT probably reported it. I was kind of upset when I called him last night, and he didn't really seem in the mood to talk. Next thing I know, you're knocking on my office door."

Her mood had become more somber by the second as she recounted everything. I felt bad about putting her through it but didn't see any way to avoid it.

"Is there any other backup for the project?"

"We have cloud backup."

"And?"

"That had been hacked and everything there was gone, too. Whoever did this knew what they were doing, and they were very thorough."

"And now you've lost three years of work."

"Thanks for reminding me."

"Maybe it can be reconstructed faster since you've been down the path once already." It was a naïve thing to say, especially given my background as an academic. You couldn't fudge results if you wanted to maintain scholarly credibility.

"The genome sequencing alone took the entire three years. I busted my ass on that." Her eyes filled with tears. "And Jack's prototype for an integrated bio refinery was about to go to the U.S. Patent Office. It would have changed the entire energy landscape—for cars, large-scale power plants, you name it. The whole project was a game changer."

For the first time since talking with Candace, my senses kicked in, my heart beat a little faster. What I had assumed was malicious hijinks by a bunch of egghead scientists now appeared to be larceny on the highest order. The reference to "commercial advances" in Dr. Wiggin's vitae and "commercial applications" in Candace's bio resurfaced in my mind.

"Let me understand this," I said. "What you were doing in the lab was creating a product that was going to be worth a lot of money?"

She nodded. "For the university, it was going to be huge. Dr. Wiggin predicted we would get a half-billion dollars in private sector money once the patent was filed. And that's just a drop in the bucket. In five years, gasoline and all petroleum-based oil products could literally be obsolete. Think about that. Monarch would change the world of energy as we know it, and also change political dynamics. Do you think we'd be sending troops over to the Middle East if we could produce all the energy we needed here on our own soil?"

It seemed like hyperbole. I'd been around enough professors who felt their research project—even the most mundane—would transform the world, earning them a Nobel and a cover photo on *Rolling Stone*.

"Tell me about your project." It was the most innocuous way I could think of to challenge her claim.

Her shoulders hunched, and she slid down in her seat. She appeared to assess me. "I don't mean to sound patronizing, but how technical do you want me to get? This is pretty advanced stuff we're working on."

"Why don't you give me the eighth-grade-science version? You know, somewhere beyond this is a microscope but this side of subatomic quark theory."

"Okay. You've heard of the human genome project, right?"

I nodded.

"Well, in addition to sequencing the genomes in humans, biologists and geneticists around the world are working on doing the same for every species in the world. My area of expertise is microbial genomics."

"Bacteria, funguses, and things like that, right?"

"Very good."

I was proud of myself for remembering the information from her bio. If this private eye thing didn't work out, maybe I could consider becoming a world-class scientist.

"Less than one one-hundredth of all microbes have been studied," she continued. "Not to pat myself on the back, but I have sequenced as many or more microbes than any other scientist in the world."

"Eleven." I patted the folder I'd consulted earlier. "Eight bacteria and three protozoa."

"Somebody has been doing a little background reading."

"I confess. Langford gave me your bio."

"I've been too busy to update it. The number's up to fourteen now."

"Busy woman."

"For all the good it's going to do me now. The last three were for this project. I had performed the sequencing for three bacteria that can convert both five- and six-carbon sugars into ethanol and recycle carbon dioxide into useful biomass."

"I'll take your word for it that this is a good thing."

"Sorry. Not eighth grade level?"

I shook my head. "I guess it's best to skip to the bottom line. What about your project would make someone want to steal it?"

"In the simplest terms, we're developing scaleable biomass fuel cells."

"Fuel cells aren't new. I mean, I first heard about fuels cells at least twenty years ago."

"Yes, true. But up until now, the problem has been how inefficient previous enzymes were to ferment sugar polymers into enzymes. Our process is ten thousand times more efficient. It truly is revolutionary."

It sounded impressive, though I wasn't sure I understood all the implications of what she was saying.

"We've proven all this in our lab studies and in some small demonstrations. Jack was able to adapt existing fuel cell technology into a creative new model. It works as well in powering a car as it does a building, or even an entire city. There are no safety or greenhouse gas issues. The cost per unit of energy is less than half of existing technology."

"So it's important and valuable."

She frowned. "You think I'm making this all up?"

"No."

"But you think I'm exaggerating."

"It doesn't matter. The fact is someone thought Monarch was worth stealing. The question I have is who knew enough about your work and its implications to think that?"

"I had no idea until about an hour ago. Now I'm pretty sure I do."

"Why, what changed an hour ago?"

She reached over and pulled a sheet of paper from her purse and handed it to me. "This is the note I mentioned earlier."

I unfolded the paper and read:

You are desecrators of Mother Earth! You have no regard for the sanctity of life on our planet, which you only want to exploit for profit, using the evil manna of corporate america to rape and destroy it. For that you must be punished. If you hope to see the return of your sinful project you will have to pay us twenty million dollars. Instructions on how to get us the money will follow. Do not contact law enforcement authorities, or we will destroy your project.

Stone Creek Saviors

The note was written in a common computer typeface on a plain sheet of paper.

"Where did you get this?"

"I found it on the windshield of my car in front of my apartment this morning."

"Did you show it to Jerry Langford?"

She shook her head. "You're the first person I've talked to since I found it. When we're done, I'm going to try calling Dr. Wiggin to let him know."

"Any idea who these Stone Creek Saviors could be?"

"I haven't had time to see if they're on the Internet, but it sounds a lot like the Students Saving Our Planet. They go by S-SOP. They're a bunch of radicals. They were suspected in last spring's firebombing of the Food Science Building, but the cops couldn't prove anything even though S-SOP had been picketing the building the day before."

"What was their issue with Food Science?"

"They conduct research on genetically modified foods. Mainly tomatoes and a few different fruits for an international food conglomerate. S-SOP was picketing to make them stop."

"And you're thinking maybe they escalated from picketing to fire-bombing?"

"Wouldn't put it past them."

"We should show Langford the note."

She hesitated. "I-I'd like to tell Dr. Wiggin first if you don't mind."

"Why?"

"It's his project. He should know before I tell the university. And, between you and me, our security department is a bunch of fuckups."

I wasn't sure if that was a good idea. Though a blowhard, Jerry Langford had hired me. "I guess I can wait a bit, but eventually we'll need to tell Langford."

"Shit!" At first I thought she was reacting to my statement, but I don't think she even heard me. She was looking through the window towards the fitness center. When I turned to look, I saw a guy in his late twenties or early thirties, a slender Asian, dressed in slacks, dress shirt, and a sport coat. He stood on the outside path and appeared to be staring at Candace.

"You know that guy?"

She nodded. "My ex. We broke up two weeks ago, and he's being a pain in the ass."

"Is he stalking you?"

"No, just being a royal jerk."

"Sorry." I wasn't sure if she wanted me to deal with him somehow or if we should just ignore him. "Is he a student?"

"Used to be. He earned his MBA last semester, and now he has his own business, but since we broke up he's…he's been coming back to campus to try and get us back together."

"What's his name?"

"Thomas. Thomas Chan."

We both glanced his way again. Chan continued to stare at us.

"Maybe we should go sit somewhere else," I said.

"No, fuck him. Oh my god, he's walking this way."

He was making his way from the path, across the grass and between a break in the shrubs, to face the full-length window in front of us. He stood about three feet away, with his arms out as if asking her "what the heck?"

Candace stood and, in one movement, threw her half-full cup of coffee against the window before turning on her heels and marching towards the exit.

three

I WATCHED HER EXIT THE café. When I looked back at the window, Chan had disappeared. I took a minute or so to pick up her paper cup and clean up what coffee I could from the floor and window. I needed more information from Candace, and I also wanted to make sure her ex-boyfriend wasn't harassing her. I hustled over to Sieboldt, finding her office closed and locked. I asked four professorial types inside Sieboldt if they'd seen her but none had. I checked a couple of labs, searched the campus grounds, and returned to the front of Sieboldt. No signs of either Candace or Chan.

The drive to Granderson had taken me forty minutes in post-rush hour traffic. I didn't want to waste the drive and return home so soon, so I went to the university library. After the student librarian made a confirming call to Langford, I was given a guest ID and password for Internet access on one of the library's computers. I typed "Thomas Chan" and "Granderson University" into the search engine and pulled up a dozen LinkedIn profiles. I ignored those and went straight to a website titled "Chan International—Thomas Chan, CEO."

The page featured a bio and a professional photo of Thomas Chan, the same guy who'd been staring down Candace Symington thirty minutes ago. I read:

> *Buoyed by an indomitable entrepreneurial spirit, President and Chief Executive Officer Thomas Chan has guided Chan International into one of the leading international manufacturing representative firms in the West. Soon after opening his firm, Mr. Chan began winning accounts in a varie-*

ty of industries, including textiles, consumer goods, high technology, energy, and automotive. The firm's clients benefit from Mr. Chan's attention to detail and negotiation skills, enabling them to reduce their production costs by an average of thirty percent, with some clients reporting savings of seventy percent!

Mr. Chan operates the firm with Vice President and Chief Operating Officer Adam Benzer. Both men received their MBA degrees from the prestigious Clifton School of Business at Granderson University in Rosetown, California. Prior to that, Mr. Chan earned a BA degree in International Studies from UCLA. He was born and raised in San Jose, California.

I went to the home page and found another photo of Chan, this one with his sleeves rolled up, tie stylishly askew, as he looked at drawings with another Asian male in what appeared to be some sort of industrial building. The home page was titled "Chan International—International Manufacturing Representatives" and was followed by a brief sales pitch to call or e-mail "for quotes on manufacturing and production for any type of product—no job is too big or too small." I read a little of Adam Benzer's bio, which was similar to Chan's—BA from UC Santa Barbara and an MBA from Granderson. One page listed some of their clients. Another page featured a couple of case studies, one for a toy manufacturer whose sole product appeared to be plastic soldiers, the other for a company producing skirts for men. I supposed that covered the consumer goods and textile industries ballyhooed in Chan's bio, though case studies of their high technology, energy, and automotive work were lacking. From what I could tell from their website, Chan International was a two-person company.

I spent another hour on the web looking for more information about Candace Symington, Ken Wiggin, and Jack Cassidy but turned up little beyond what Langford had given me in the file. I searched for microbial fuel cells and microbial genome sequencing, finding several links to academic articles. I read a few of them but gained no new insights. None of these searches pulled up anything on the fuel cell work being done at Granderson. Apparently, Wiggin's team had done a good job of keeping things under wraps.

By the time I left the library, rain was falling. Wearing just a light coat, I began a brisk walk to my car, eager to turn on the heater and return home for lunch.

Thomas Chan stood next to my car holding aloft a black umbrella. He'd donned a long raincoat since I'd last seen him outside the café. The increasing rain did nothing to break the cold stare he gave me.

"I'd pay you for trying to keep my car dry with your umbrella, but all I've got is a credit card."

"Excuse me?"

"Umbrella. Car." I pointed at each object. "You standing there. It's a joke. Not a good one."

"You've got a smart mouth for an old white guy."

"Fifty is the new forty. But in my case, it might be the new thirty-five. I used to be quite the gym rat. Feel that." I made a muscle with my right arm and pointed at my biceps.

"What were you doing with my girlfriend?"

I had a good four inches on him and thirty pounds, but he looked athletic enough for me to be wary. "Last I heard, she was your ex-girlfriend. And she doesn't appreciate you following her around campus. As you noted yourself, I've been around the block a few times, so let me tell you, women don't dig the lovesick puppy types. It's a bit pathetic."

"Shut up."

"I'd like to stick around and listen to more of your witty come-backs, but it's starting to rain pretty hard and I don't have a nifty Ralph Lauren umbrella like you do."

"I don't know who you are, but you're to stay away from her."

"Why did you two break up anyway? Oh wait, don't tell me, I bet she thought you were too possessive and too jealous. Sound about right?"

"That business is between she and I."

"Her and me. It should be 'between her and me,' not 'she and I.' But that's beside the point. So I actually have a business question for you. How can I go about ordering one of those man skirts you guys make?"

Chan blinked, surprised at the reference to his business. "We don't make anything. We represent overseas manufacturers and onshore companies."

"Point well taken. But the question remains, how do I get a skirt thing?"

"Have you been cyber-stalking me?"

"That's a bit dramatic. I've been doing research."

"Well, don't."

"Or what? You'll give me a knuckle sandwich?"

"A what?"

"Knuckle sandwich. It's a euphemism for a punch to the face. It's a bit cliché and…oh, never mind." I shouldered my way past Chan and got into my car and out of the rain. As I drove away, I watched him in my rearview mirror, standing under his umbrella, glaring at me.

four

EVERY SEAT IN THE NELSON Medical Group's large waiting room was taken. After I checked in with the receptionist, paid the twenty-dollar co-pay, and found a recent edition of *Golf Magazine*, I located a wall to lean against and thumb through the magazine. With spring still a month away, most of the patients—sniffling, honking, or moaning—appeared afflicted with one form or another of a cold or flu. My position against the wall kept as much distance as possible from the sickest of the lot.

Leafing through the magazine, replete with images of lush golf courses, elegantly engineered golf clubs and gear, and tips on how to shoot in the seventies, had me considering returning to the sport. I'd been a pretty good golfer in my younger days, having won a couple of tournaments as an undergraduate on the San Jose State University men's golf team. As my career and family commitments grew over the years, the number of rounds I played declined. It had been eight or nine years since I'd last played. As I was becoming engrossed in a story about the best public course in the United States, a woman opened the door leading to the back offices and called my name.

I followed her past four or five closed doors to a scale, where I weighed in. She led me to a private room, and I sat on the examination table as instructed. She asked some basic questions about diet, exercise, and my general health before leaving me alone to wait for the doctor.

After ten minutes, I wished I'd brought the *Golf Magazine* with me. During the wait, I considered whether I should have come or not. I wasn't sick. I didn't have any aches or pains. Before I could summon enough momentum to rise from the table and walk out, in walked Dr. Albert Nelson.

He greeted me and looked through the folder the nurse had left for him. "What's going on?"

"I don't know, but I think I might have some mental things happening."

"Mental things? Can you tell me what you mean by that?" He sat down on a rolling stool across from me.

"I can't get certain things out of my mind. They won't go away."

"Go on."

I took a deep breath. "I...I was involved in some extreme violence not too long ago. A shootout. People were killed. That's what I keep seeing. The horrors of that. And the guilt that comes with it."

"I read about...about what happened. Four dead men. Terrible thing, but it sounded like you didn't have much choice. Isn't that right?"

"Doesn't make it easier. I still see what happened vividly in my mind. Sometimes I swear I can even smell the lingering gunpowder."

"Have you had any physical symptoms?" Dr. Nelson looked at me closely.

"Sometimes. My heart speeds up when the images come. Not every time but when I let myself dwell on it. A couple of times I felt myself hyperventilating, and I had to lie down to calm myself."

When he finished writing, he looked me in the eyes. "What you went through would trouble anybody. That's a normal reaction to that kind of trauma. We all process something like that in our own way. Your mind is doing that now, trying to put into context something alien to your psyche."

I nodded. He wasn't telling me anything I didn't already know, but it was good to hear it from him anyway. Somehow that made me feel better.

"My concern," he continued, "is the persistence of these visions, and the emotions they're arousing, might be a sign of post-traumatic stress disorder. PTSD."

"I'm usually pretty strong about facing things, even unpleasant things—"

He held up a hand to quiet me. "PTSD is not a sign of weakness or anything like that. It's your mind's normal reaction. Your mind might be able to deal with things in a few weeks, and you'll move on and be fine. Or these visions could haunt you for months or years. Or they might never go away."

"So I've got that going for me."

"Yes, you do." Dr. Nelson granted me a smile. "In cases like this, however, we don't like to take chances. It's best we treat you for the PTSD symptoms earlier rather than later. How long ago did you say the events took place?"

"November."

"So it's been about three months." Dr. Nelson looked at me with evident concern.

"Yeah."

"Okay, here's what we're going to do." He pulled out a prescription pad from his shirt pocket. "First of all, I want to get you started on Zoloft. We'll start with twenty-five milligrams and see how it works. It'll take a couple of weeks for you to start feeling the effects."

"An anti-depressant?" I didn't want to go on medications.

"This is a low dose," he said, detecting my reticence. "Given what you've told me, I think this would be helpful for you."

"I don't know," I protested, but I took the prescription when he handed it to me. "I don't want to start down that path, you know, of taking medicine for every little thing ailing me. At my age, the meds could add up pretty fast."

"I don't consider PTSD to be a little thing. Please get the prescription filled and begin using it, today if possible. As I said, it will take a couple of weeks before it starts to work."

"Will this help me sleep better?" I held up the prescription.

"Yes. I'm also going to give you a referral for a psychiatrist. You can use anybody listed on our HMO website, but I recommend you consider Dr. Frank Beckly. He specializes in PTSD. I've had several patients see him, and they all swear by him. He utilizes trauma-focused cognitive-behavioral therapy. Therapy combined with the Zoloft should start to help you."

"What is trauma-focused, whatever it is you said?"

"He'll explain it in detail to you, but it's basically getting you to open up and express what's happening to you and to develop strategies for dealing with it. It's an interactive treatment model. He's used it a lot with war veterans."

five

AFTER MY DOCTOR'S APPOINTMENT, I called Jerry Langford to get an address for Jack Cassidy, Candace Symington's fellow researcher on the Monarch project. I was surprised the Sacramento address belonged to an establishment called The Zoo that, according to its sign, opened at six in the morning and closed at two in the morning, enabling customers to take full advantage of the state's legal drinking hours. At eight at night, the bar's parking lot was full. A look inside revealed The Zoo catered to a middle-aged crowd that long ago exited the fast track for a barstool planted on Cirrhosis Island. To call the place a dive would have been a compliment, as stretched as calling Danny DeVito a hunk.

A dozen or so men and maybe five women sat at the bar while another ten to fifteen customers drank in the booths lining the wall a few feet behind. The place was no bigger than a storage shed and just as dark, the decorating motif "beer signs of the 1970s." It smelled of Lysol and sounded like dashed dreams—laughs too loud, voices too slurred, opinions of others too ready.

"I'm looking for Jack Cassidy," I said to the bartender. There was no room at the bar, so I stood at the station where the cocktail waitress ordered and retrieved her drinks.

"Yeah, what do you want?" The man was pushing sixty years old and two hundred fifty pounds. He was bald, with a drinker's nose and a cigarette smoker's voice. The white apron he wore had been unlaundered since Richard Nixon's presidency.

"*You're* Jack Cassidy?"

"Like I said, what do you want?"

"You're the PhD student at Granderson University?"

I felt a jab in my back, not hard but insistent. "Out of the way, pal." It was the cocktail waitress reclaiming her station. She wore frizzy blond hair, a clownish amount of makeup, a low-scooped white shirt revealing most of her breasts, and silver hot pants so short and tight they could have been painted on. All of this might have been fine had the waitress not been about seventy, missing two top teeth, and weighing about ninety-five pounds, her flesh fish belly white.

"I'm sorry, ma'am." I moved to the side behind a large guy sitting at the last barstool next to the workstation.

"Don't worry about it, sweetie. Can I get you something to drink?"

"Sure," I said after a pause. "Gin and tonic."

"Want to make it a double? Double's only a buck more if you order from the well."

"Why not?" By now Jack had moved to the other end of the bar. I figured it might be a few minutes before he'd make his way back and we could talk. Besides, I felt bad about encroaching on the waitress's territory. Ordering a drink was the least I could do.

She lifted a leaf in the bar and went to the bartender side. She poured me more than a double, added a lime wedge, and slid the drink my way. I had to reach around the big guy to retrieve it.

The gin and tonic tasted mainly of gin. After the first few tentative sips, I managed to power through half of it.

"Let me make sure I'm clear on this," I said. "You work and study at the university?"

He laughed as he was pulling two beers out from the refrigerator underneath the bar. "No, I never said that. Do I look like I work at the university?"

"I was given this address for Jack Cassidy. I guess they gave me the wrong Jack Cassidy." I silently cursed Jerry Langford.

I finished my drink, put a ten on the bar and started to leave.

"Why you looking for Jack Cassidy?" the bartender said over the din.

"University business." I walked back closer to the bar.

"He in trouble or something?"

"No. Not that I know of. I'm trying to help him and his colleagues with a little problem."

"You're not a cop?" He looked me up and down and his manner changed from brusque bartender to something else—curious, maybe protective.

"No."

He continued to look at me, taking inventory. "He's upstairs. Jack's my son. I didn't catch your name."

I introduced myself and told him I had talked with Candace Symington earlier in the day and now wanted to follow up with Jack. He still seemed suspicious, but he gave me directions to the stairs outside leading to the apartment above The Zoo. I thanked him and left, feeling his eyes follow me until the door closed behind me.

Cassidy opened the door before I'd finished climbing the stairs, no doubt given a heads-up by his father. He stood maybe five ten and weighed a hundred seventy pounds or so. His straight light-brown hair fell over his ears and forehead almost to his eyes, a hairstyle you might expect to find on a middle-schooler rather than a PhD.

"Ray Courage?"

I nodded. "Nice of your dad to give me an introduction."

He smiled. "Candace called earlier, too. Said you might come by. I'd be glad to talk, but I don't have a lot of time." He stepped away from the door to let me enter.

It was a studio, about what you'd expect to find above a place like The Zoo. A single bed, a couch covered with a bed sheet, a flat screen television, and an old kitchen table with three unmatched chairs comprised the furnishings. There was room for little else except a tiny kitchen with a sink, stove, and a mini fridge. The muted voices of the customers at The Zoo wafted up through the floorboards, as did the unmistakable aroma of stale beer.

We sat at the table, and I declined his offer for coffee.

"Candace says you're a private investigator. What makes you think you can help us?"

"I'm not sure I can, to be honest."

Because of the inadequate heat inside his apartment, he wore a white hoodie and a black baseball cap emblazoned with a T.

"Cal Tech baseball," he said, noticing me puzzling over his ball cap.

"I couldn't figure it out. I thought I knew the designs and logos of pretty much every pro and college team around. I didn't know Cal Tech had a baseball team."

He laughed. "If you could call it that. Worst team in all of college baseball. In my four years we didn't win a single game. Never even came close. A bad high school team could have beaten us."

"School like Cal Tech, it's got to be hard to recruit good athletes. No offense."

"That's just it. They don't recruit athletes at all. But the administration wanted us to be well rounded, so we were required to play a varsity sport. I picked baseball because I was an okay left-handed pitcher in Little League. In college? Not so much. But you aren't here to listen about my glorious athletic career, and I do need to leave pretty soon."

"Hot date?"

"Something like that."

"Let's get to it then. What can you tell me about the theft of your project?"

"Candace probably told you everything I can tell you."

"Why's it called Monarch? Just curious."

"That's our working name for the project. When we file the patent and publish the paper the name will be about as long as my arm, so for simplicity we called it the Monarch Project. That is, if we ever recover the damn thing." His words came fast, though I didn't know him well enough to attribute that to nerves or his normal speaking style.

"But why Monarch?"

"Didn't Candace tell you something about it?"

"A little. Something about microbial genomes and biofuel cells."

"So you have a basic idea of at least the elements of the project. Two of the three microbes that will power my biofuel cell come from the waste matter from the species *Danaus plexippus*, better known as the Monarch butterfly."

"Clever," I said, sounding more dismissive than I'd intended.

"We're scientists and engineers, not ad copywriters."

"Sorry."

He fidgeted, picked up the cell phone on the table, glanced at a message or the time or something, then got up and went over to the refrigerator. He pulled out a bottle of water. "Want one?"

"Thanks."

He handed me a plastic bottle as he returned to his seat at the table. He took a long drink of water from his own bottle and set it down next to his phone.

"Who do you think took your work?"

He shrugged. "From the note Candace got, it sounds like the Stone Creek Saviors. Whoever they are."

"What about S-SOP?" I asked.

"I don't know. But nobody outside the project and our investors knew what we were working on. We were a small, tight group. I don't see how S-SOP or these Stone Creek Saviors would have known what we were doing. Even if they did, I don't know why they would take our project. It's an environmentally positive technology."

"Maybe they want twenty million dollars."

He snorted. "Good old-fashioned greed. I guess that never goes out of style."

"Professor Wiggin, Candace, and you are all on the project. Who else?"

"I guess you could say we're the big three. Wiggin oversees the overall project, though his main emphasis is dealing with the administration and keeping our work funded. Candace heads up the biological side of things while I head the engineering. She and I each have several grad students—masters candidates—but we've been particular about partitioning their awareness and knowledge of the project."

"Partitioning. How do you mean?"

"We give each of them a specific assignment. So, for example, if I have five grad students, I give each one a small piece of the puzzle to figure out. One student gets puzzle A, one gets puzzle B, and so on. When all the little puzzles are solved, I put them together to assemble the overall puzzle. Candace does more or less the same thing. My explanation is a bit simplistic, but in a nutshell it's how we do things."

Something didn't sound right about this. I thought about it as I took a sip of water.

"With all due respect, the way Candace described your team's work it sounds like you may be creating a new energy future and solving global warming. How can a team of three people, plus maybe a dozen grunt grad students, accomplish that when there are large corporations and research labs around the world who've been unable to do it?"

He smiled. "Candace might have overstated our accomplishment a tad bit. I mean, yes, what Monarch has uncovered—and appears to be on the threshold of introducing—can ease our dependence on petroleum. But that path is a long and slippery one."

"Still, you've done something scores if not hundreds of researchers have been trying—"

"We got lucky or we're brilliant. Take your pick. All those other researchers you're talking about have been close. What they were missing was the genome sequencing we've been holding onto. With the sequencing, I was able to engineer something unique. It doesn't take a thousand people to do that."

There was no reason to debate the point. My job was to get the project back, not to evaluate its merits.

"Is it possible one of your grad students took it? Or maybe a professor at a different school? Or someone else who maybe guessed what you're working on?"

"I doubt the students could have figured it out. Only Candace, Dr. Wiggin, and I have seen the full genome sequences. We've been careful about that. And they aren't sophisticated enough to hack into our security or brazen enough to steal the server. The one possibility I can think of is Truxel Laboratories over in Davis. Dr. Wiggin has a friend there who is doing similar work on biofuel cells. A few months ago, Ken—Dr. Wiggin—said he'd talked to this guy about how we were about to patent our fuel cell design. Ken slipped and told him about Candace's genome sequencing breakthrough. Candace and I were upset he did that. Ken said it didn't matter because this guy didn't have the actual sequence."

"Do you happen to know this guy's name at Truxel?"

"Corey Truxel. It's his company. The guy's been around forever, though he hasn't done anything groundbreaking since the nineties."

"I'm surprised Dr. Wiggin would leak information about Monarch to a potential competitor like that."

Cassidy forced a laugh. "You shouldn't be."

"What do you mean?"

"Dr. Wiggin is a bit, um, different. Not what most people expect from a distinguished professor in his seventies."

"Care to elaborate?"

He shook his head. "See for yourself. Ken will be back in town the day after tomorrow. Talk to him and then tell me if you're still surprised he talked out of turn."

"What's he doing in Germany anyway?"

"I don't know. He said it was part business, part personal. He was attending some conference. And he has some family in Baden Baden." His water half-finished, Cassidy stood. "I don't mean to be rude, but I have to get going."

I took a final sip of water, screwed the top back on the bottle, and took it with me as I left. As I headed down the stairs, I heard the firm click of a deadbolt behind me.

six

THAT EVENING AFTER DINNER—beef stew I'd started in the morning and cooked all day in the crockpot—I settled in at the computer. I found three articles about the firebombing the previous spring at Granderson University. The first, a digest item in the *Sacramento Bee*, consisted of three short paragraphs offering little more than the what, when, and where of the incident. The Rosetown daily paper had a few more details and a photograph of the damage to the exterior of the building, but it offered little insight as to who might have been behind the bombing. The online student newspaper for Granderson University, *The Griffin Speaks*, was the longest and best story of the three.

Food Science Building Attacked

by Katie Johnson

Early this morning, an unknown arsonist threw a Molotov cocktail through the glass front door of the Food Science Building on campus.

The fire burned the floor and one wall of the building's entryway, while smoke damaged three original paintings. Campus officials estimated the damage at about $25,000. Damage might have been worse, according to the Rosetown Fire Chief Tim Nakashima, had the breaking of the front door glass not set off an alarm, alerting campus security, who arrived at the scene minutes later and summoned the fire department.

Campus Chief of Security Jerry Langford condemned the terrorist attack and vowed to bring to justice those responsible.

"This is a very unfortunate occurrence," he said. "Granderson is a safe haven. For an individual or a group of individuals to threaten that sense of security of our students, faculty, and staff is an outrage."

Though Langford would not comment further on the subject, he did acknowledge that the "SCS" initials spray-painted on the side of the building near where the attack occurred could be that of an eco-terrorist organization known as Stone Creek Saviors.

Students Saving Our Earth, or S-SOP, had picketed the Food Science Building the day before. The group was protesting the Food Science Department's research of genetically modified foods. Much of that research is funded by Alton & Grayton Corporation, the world's largest food processing conglomerate.

"They got what they deserved, man," said Seth Seeger, president of S-SOP's Granderson chapter, who was on the scene to watch the fire department put out the flames. He denied accusations S-SOP had anything to do with the firebombing or that his organization was connected to the Stone Creek Saviors.

"Genetically modified foods, or Frankenstein food, is a threat to all of us. For the university to encourage research in that area is unconscionable," he said.

Langford said his department would continue to review tapes from nearby security cameras for clues in identifying the culprits, but so far nothing has turned up.

Anyone with information about the attack is asked to call Granderson campus security at 530-555-1257.

It took all of five minutes to find a cell phone number for Seth Seeger. He picked up right away. I identified myself as an investigator on the Food Science arson and said his name had come up as part of an investigation.

"That's bullshit, man." He had a nasally voice steeped with petulance. "I already talked to the police last spring. Campus security, too. I didn't do shit."

"I know it, you know it. So why don't we clear your name once and for all so you don't have to keep getting hassled."

"How do we do that?"

"Let me get a full and complete statement for my report. I'll declare you free and clear of the matter, and it'll be over."

"Now? On the phone?"

"No, are you free now? How about I buy you a beer?" Rule One in the Ray Courage Manual, use alcohol to ingratiate yourself to hostile individuals.

"I guess. If you're sure this will end all the bullshit."

"I believe it will." I gave him the address of the Fahrenheit 250 Restaurant across from Sac State and asked him to meet me there in an hour.

Fahrenheit 250 was the latest inhabitant of the building on Folsom Boulevard. Their proximity to a large urban university notwithstanding, the restaurants and bars occupying the building over the previous twenty years had come and gone with little success, despite having a full liquor license, usually a magnet for college students. Because Sac State was essentially a commuter school, most students returned to their own neighborhoods when drinking hours commenced, rendering the area in and around the campus a ghost town after classes ended.

Fahrenheit 250 appeared to be doing better than most of its predecessors, having survived its first two years of business, a strong review in the *Bee,* and its appeal to both families and college students contributing to its endurance. The restaurant derived its name from the temperature at which it slow-cooked its meats—ribs, tri-tip, pork, and chicken.

On this night at about nine o'clock, several families ate in the large dining area, many of the teen and pre-teen kids wearing soccer or baseball uniforms; a night out for dinner was an easy choice for parents who had to work all day and then shuttle kids to and from ballgames. At the bar, four guys attempted to flirt with three women in their early twenties. I sat at one of the vacant tables in the bar. Seth Seeger was late.

I started on my second beer when a skinny kid with curly brown hair down to his shoulders walked in. He had a moderate case of acne and wore a T-shirt decorated with the words "You are not an environmentalist if you eat factory farmed animals." He might as well have had "Seth Seeger" tattooed on his forehead.

I waved him over.

"Beer?" I asked.

He nodded. "Anything non-American."

I went to the bar and ordered him a Heineken. He looked at it with disdain when I handed it to him at the table.

"So what's your deal?" he asked when I'd settled back into my chair.

"Like I said on the phone, I'm trying to tie up loose ends on the arson."

"Are you some sort of arson specialist or something? I thought the investigation was over and they never found out who did it."

"Who do you think did it?"

"How the hell would I know?"

"What about the Stone Creek Saviors?"

"Ask them."

"Aren't the Saviors and S-SOP like brothers in arms?"

"No." He snorted. "The Saviors are eco-terrorists, man. S-SOP is a student organization. We're not into violence."

"How was it you happened on the Food Science Building a few minutes after it'd been torched last spring?"

"Coincidence. I was in the library studying and was heading for my car when I heard the sirens."

I drank some of my beer, an Eel River Pale Ale. "In the Granderson paper, you said the research going on at Food Science was creating 'Frankenstein food.'"

"So? That's what they're doing. Who knows what damage they're doing to people who eat their genetically altered crap." He took a tentative sip of beer. "Aren't you going to take notes or something?"

"No need," I said, tapping my temple with an index finger. "Like a steel trap."

"Whatever. As long as you people quit hassling me after tonight."

"Have you heard the term 'Frankenstein Labs' used at Granderson?"

"Of course, that's what they call Professor Wiggin's lab. It's because he's crazy as a loon. And because their work's a big freaking secret for some reason."

"Do you know what they're doing over there?"

"No. It's a big secret, like I said."

"There must be rumors, or people who think they know."

He laughed to himself and then drank more beer. After he swallowed, he moved his lips in and out as if trying to get rid of the taste. "Forrester thinks they're working on a new system for fracking. He says they're getting money from Sunrise Oil. Corporate pigs." He blushed, as if he'd said something he hadn't meant to.

"Who's Forrester?"

"No one. Never mind."

"Is he in S-SOP?"

"I said never mind."

"Or is he in Stone Creek Saviors?"

"I don't know what you're talking about. Why are you asking me about Wiggin's shit? I thought you were investigating the arson?"

"Just trying to put everything into context."

"Whatever."

"Do you know anybody who works over at Sieboldt?"

He shook his head. "Man, I've taken one science class my entire time at Granderson. Introduction to biology my freshman year. I haven't set foot in Sieboldt since. I'm a sociology major. I hang out on the other side of campus."

"Do you have an opinion on what goes on at Sieboldt?"

He exhaled in frustration. "I don't have any idea what you're getting at. Do I have an opinion? Yeah, I have an opinion. The shit that goes on in Sieboldt or Frankenstein or whatever you want to call it is the same shit that goes on in every other department at Granderson. It's all about money. They'll take any corporate dollar they can get and then do whatever research the money men tell them to. It's just as bad in the sociology department as it is in Sieboldt. Everyone's making money. Everyone but the students."

I let him finish, deciding to wait a few extra seconds to let him calm down. When I started to ask him another question, he interrupted me.

"This is bullshit," he said. "Thanks for the crappy beer." He stood and stormed out.

So much for Rule One and ingratiating myself to hostile individuals.

seven

I SAT INSIDE MY CAR in front of Thomas Chan's house. The brick home in McKinley Park featured a sloping shingle roof, arched doorway, and double-paned windows. It wasn't huge, though it probably had at least three bedrooms and a couple of bathrooms. For this part of town, the price tag on a house like this pushed a million dollars. I wondered if he owned or rented the place. Either way, he'd have a steep monthly payment on his hands.

After about ten minutes, Rubia arrived and parked behind me. I exited my car and waited for her to approach.

"It's about time." I tapped my watch.

"You want me to leave?"

"No, late or not, I'm stuck with you."

"Yeah, stuck. As in, I'm bailing out your sorry ass yet again."

A minute later, Chan flung the door open just after we rang his doorbell.

"What the hell do you want?" He glowered at me, nostrils flaring. He glanced at Rubia, looked her up and down, and returned the smile she gave him. Given our earlier run-in, I knew I needed something to change the contentious dynamic between Chan and me. That was why I'd asked Rubia to join me.

Chan was a good-looking guy, fashionably under-dressed in skinny cargo pants and a ribbed purple Armani sweater that probably cost four bills. Maybe he didn't have the coin for a Rolex, but he did sport a classic Baume & Mercier wristwatch.

"Thomas, I know we didn't get off to such a great start yesterday. My name's Ray Courage. I'm an investigator, and I've been asked by the university to look into an incident at Sieboldt Science Center. This is my colleague, Rubia. Rubia, this is Thomas Chan." I was laying on the civility, my need for information outweighing my disdain for the prick.

"So nice to meet you." Pretty and petite, Rubia could bring the charm when needed. Never mind that she'd once commanded the most ruthless street gang in Northern California.

"Hi." Chan's right hand was wrapped in a bandage the size of a kitchen mitt, an addition since our encounter the day before.

"What happened to your hand?" she asked.

"Nothing." He winced as he put the hand behind his back.

"We're sorry to bother you at home," Rubia continued. She was working her charm, sounding more like a soccer mom than an ex-gangbanger. "But we're working on something for the university and thought maybe you could help us." She reached out with her hand and gently touched Chan's non-bandaged left forearm.

He thought for a second. "I don't have a lot of time. I'm working from home today." He stepped back and let us inside.

For someone right out of grad school, Chan's furnishings were impressive. Everything in the living room where we sat appeared to be chosen and coordinated by someone with a professional eye. And deep pockets.

"Nice," I said, looking around the room before giving him my sincerest insincere smile.

Rubia had done her part by placating Chan and getting us inside. Now, I had to get some answers. Chan settled into a sofa seat in the living room, and Rubia and I sat at opposite ends of the couch.

"You didn't come here to admire my home. So what do you want to know?" Chan had a nervous energy about him. I'd seen his type before, a young man who couldn't wait to make his first million dollars and keep on going from there.

I held my fake smile a few more seconds before I spoke. "Do you know much about the work being done by Dr. Wiggin and his team over at Sieboldt?"

"You mean Candace's project? No, I don't know a thing about it."

"She's never said anything about it to you? Not even casually?"

"No, because I don't care anything about her work."

His answers came quickly, preemptive salvos to cut off that conversational path. He had the self-assured air of someone who considered himself the smartest guy in every room he graced.

"What do you know about S-SOP?" I asked.

He snorted. "Bunch of environmental wackos. Especially their so-called leader, Seth Seeger."

"Why do you think he's a wacko?"

"Because the asshole threatened us—Chan International—a few months ago. He sent Adam and me an e-mail using all his left-wing environmental rhetoric."

"What did the e-mail say?"

"You know, the usual bullshit these weirdos spout. About how we were capitalist pigs, desecrators of the earth, out to rape and destroy the land, and so on."

Some of the words he recounted were the same as those in the note Candace had shown me the day before. "Why was S-SOP so mad at your company?"

"*Pfhfft!* Because we do a lot of business with Chinese companies. They said we were supporting companies known to be the worst polluters on the planet."

That made some sense to me. "How did they know about your company? Have you ever met Seth or anyone in S-SOP?"

"No. They probably read the story in the Granderson student newspaper a few months back. It talked about the success of our company and what our business was all about."

"You said S-SOP threatened you. What did they say?"

"Nothing concrete. Something like if we don't stop we'll be sorry. Very sophomoric. It was pretty much like the note I found on my car a week before that."

"A note from S-SOP."

"No, they signed it SCS. But it was the same rhetoric, not word for word, but close enough." When he stopped talking, he recoiled in pain, grabbing his right arm with his left hand and bending forward until his upper body was parallel with the floor.

"That looks like it hurts," Rubia said. "Can I do something?"

Chan shook his head as he returned to a normal sitting position. His eyes were watery, his face pale.

I pointed at the bandage.

"I cut it on a broken bottle." He stared at me, jaw tight.

"I hate it when that happens." I kept my eyes locked on his. "Can I see the e-mail?"

"What e-mail?"

"The one from S-SOP, threatening you."

"I deleted it the same day I got it." He looked away. "I figured it was some dumb kids trying to act tough. And I was right. They haven't done anything since."

"What about the note?"

"I tossed it in a trash can."

"Did you think about maybe showing it to the police?"

"No. Bunch of stupid punks. Like I said, nothing's happened since."

I looked at his bandaged hand and considered his statement. "Let's go back to your dealings with Candace."

"Dealings? You mean my relationship with her?"

"Yes." I glanced over at Rubia, hoping she might jump into the conversation.

"I don't want to talk about that. It's personal. And none of your business."

"Fair enough. What's your take on the work they're doing over at Sieboldt? Some people say they're developing breakthrough technologies. What do you think?"

"Like I said, I don't know anything about what she does." He was stonewalling me, crossing his arms to emphasize the subject was closed.

I pushed him a couple more times about his knowledge of the work at Sieboldt, but he wouldn't budge. He said he knew nothing and stuck to it. Even Rubia's charming presence had its limits as Chan grew impatient and shuttled us out the door before we could get anything else out of him.

"Think that sucka told us the truth about those S-SOP dudes sending him an e-mail?" Rubia asked as we stood on the sidewalk in front of Chan's house.

"Probably," I said. "He's got no reason to make up something about that. Same with the note on his car. Though, if you'd been on your game, we might have been able to talk to him longer."

"Hell, if it wasn't for me, you wouldn't have gotten jack but a door slammed in your face."

"True." I looked back at Chan's house. "What do you make of his bandage?"

"Don't know. Didn't cut it on a beer bottle, though."

We went to our separate cars and drove off. I made it to the end of Chan's street and turned right when my cell phone started playing *La Bamba*, Rubia's ringtone.

"Yeah."

"Ray, drive around the block and go by Chan's house again. I'll follow."

"Why? What's going on?"

"Just do it. I need to check something out."

I made three more right turns to get back to Chan's street. Except for the same couple of cars parked on the side of the street, I saw nothing of interest.

"See the black Chevy Camaro up on the right?" she asked over the phone. "Don't look at it when you drive by. Just keep going. I'll check it out and get the plate number."

"What do you think—"

"Do it, Ray. Trust me."

I did as instructed, though I sneaked a glance at the car as I drew even with it. The driver's window was rolled down. An Asian man of about thirty, wearing a big pair of sunglasses, sat behind the wheel, his meaty arm resting on the door's open window. I turned away before I could tell if he saw me looking.

After we turned off of Chan's street, Rubia spoke again. "Golden Dragons."

"What?"

"The punk in the car is a Golden Dragon. They're old-school Asian bangers. They go way back. Started in San Francisco, then moved down to LA. Heard they were starting up something in Sacramento, but that's the first I've seen of them."

"You're sure this guy's one of them?"

"Yeah. He must be a boss or some other big shit. Dragons like Chevys and Fords. The street punks drive older low-riders. The top guys like the brand new Camaros like that one. And the dude had a big diamond stud in his left ear. Another sign."

"You think Thomas Chan is hanging out with drug dealers?"

"Not drug dealers. Golden Dragons are more than that. They push drugs, sure, but they're into shaking down mom and pops, loan sharking, prostitution, gambling, and financial crimes. They're diversified gangstas."

I knew better than to question Rubia's ability to identify a gang member. She'd run a gang. Her non-profit, It's My Life, or IML as they called it, worked with kids to steer them away from the gang life. If anyone knew how to spot a gangster, she did.

Now I had to figure out what it meant.

eight

ONCE I LEFT CHAN'S HOUSE, I made a couple of calls on a small case for an insurance client and then headed to Old Sacramento to meet Danny Cashmore for lunch at the Firehouse. Danny greeted me with a bear hug. He and I had been college roommates all four years at San Jose State. We didn't see each other much anymore, having lunch maybe once every two years. Danny preferred the card tables at Lake Tahoe and big-ticket golf in Carmel, the former activity outside my interest, the latter beyond my pocketbook. The son of an Acura car dealer in Santa Clara, Danny used the old man's acumen, not to mention his bankroll, to grow four thriving dealerships of his own in Sacramento. At present he owned three—Toyota, Lexus and Subaru dealerships—the fourth dealership had long-since been turned over to wife number three. With her sense of humor intact after the divorce, she renamed the dealership Goldigger's Ford.

Danny and I exchanged small talk for a while before he came to the reason why I'd been invited to lunch. "I need to engage your professional services."

"Which services would those be?"

"Your investigation services, smart ass."

The waiter arrived, and Danny ordered a glass of Merlot and I ordered a Hendrick's martini, up with two olives. It had been a while since I'd eaten at the Firehouse, which was built as an actual firehouse in 1850. After decades of neglect, the wrecking ball was about to finish the place off when an entrepreneur bought it in 1960 and transformed it into one of Sacramento's most elegant restaurants. It was very old school. The main dining area in which we sat featured brick walls painted off-white, with gilt-framed mirrors and paintings on every wall. Red-and-gold patterned upholstered booths and chairs were right out of the late nineteenth century, while three large flower arrangements provided accents of color and more contemporary charm. The dining room was about half-filled, skewing more towards the wealthy business crowd than the young hipsters who frequented most of the other restaurants in Old Town.

"All right. Tell me what you've got."

"I need you to do a background check on someone."

"A background check? Danny, you know as well as I do there are companies who do nothing but background checks on employees. You must use them all the time for your dealerships."

He shook his head and started to explain when the waiter showed up with our drinks. After he set them down we ordered lunch. Danny went for the rib eye while I opted for the fish tacos with a mango, avocado, and cucumber slaw.

"It isn't an employee I need you to check into." He took a sip of his wine. "You know, I've had bit of bad luck when it's come to choosing spousal units."

"Spousal units? Maybe that's part of your problem right there. Spousal units."

"Just a term. I've been married three times, divorced three times. Hell, you were best man at the first two of them, and you would have been for the third but we got married spur of the moment in Thailand." He shook his head, recalling something from that experience.

"Yeah, yeah, I know all this. I told you numbers one and two were a mistake from the get-go, but you never listened to me." I sampled the martini, the Hendrick's rich and smooth. I took a bigger sip. "Number three, Debbie, now she I liked. Good sense of humor, smart."

"Yeah, smart. Smart enough to take me to the cleaners in the divorce. And that's why I need you. I'm thinking about getting married again. Call me a fool, but I like being married."

"No, you like *getting* married. I'm not so sure about *being* married."

"Ha ha."

"You want me to do a background check on a potential wife? Wife number four?"

"Yes."

"I can't do that. It sounds too, well, sleazy."

"She won't have to know. I can't risk another messy divorce and losing half my ass in the process. I want this one to work out."

"Do a pre-nup."

"Pre-nups are a kiss of death. It's like saying 'I do' with your fingers crossed. No pre-nups. Come on, Ray, do this for me."

I drank more of the gin. Here I was getting my arm twisted by a car salesman. There was little doubt in my mind who'd win our verbal tug of war. "Who is she?"

"Atta boy! And lunch is on me. I met her at my country club, Sacramento Oaks. Her name's Jolene Gillingwater. She's the general manager of the place. A real looker, smart, funny, and with common sense. We've been dating a couple of months, and I think I'm ready to pop the question, but first I want to make sure. You know what I mean?"

I told him I'd give him a discounted rate, but he wouldn't have it. "I've got someone who helps me out in my work from time to time. I might need her for some for this." I was thinking of Rubia. She could use a few extra bucks and might find the work more stimulating than I would. "I've got something going now that might take up some of my time."

We finished lunch, and after I told him I'd report back in a week, we parted company. I called Rubia from my car and briefed her on the assignment. I'd get the background check started on Jolene Gillingwater and then turn it over to Rubia for any needed follow up.

"Are you cool, Ray?" Rubia asked after I'd finished running through the plan for the background check.

"Yeah, fine. Why?"

"You just seem different...since November. Like you're lost in your own head sometimes."

"You're imagining things. Don't worry about me." I didn't feel good about shutting Rubia out like that. She was there at the shootout. It had affected me. She had to know that. She just couldn't know how. We'd been friends a long time now, ever since she first set foot in my class at Sacramento State. I'd been her first college professor after she left prison and decided to stop the gangbanging lifestyle that had sent her there. She went from a gangbanger to a college graduate who ran a respectable bar and operated a worthy non-profit. I liked and respected Rubia. But I didn't want to share with her what had been going through my mind. At least not until I'd sorted it out myself.

"You're bullshitting me. I don't like that."

My phone beeped. Caller ID indicated Regal Systems. "I have to take this call." I clicked Rubia off and answered.

nine

I DIDN'T RECOGNIZE MOST OF the company names listed on the "Current Clients" page on Chan International's website. Two company names did stand out. The first, Regal Systems, was a Sacramento manufacturer of plastic pipe, fittings, and valves. They were one of the area's largest employers and had been in the news because they were angling for tax breaks from the city of Sacramento by threatening to move to Reno. The second company was SMUD, an acronym for the Sacramento Municipal Utility District. SMUD wasn't a company per se, but rather a municipality owned by the people of Sacramento. They generated, transmitted, and distributed electricity to every home and business in the county, racking up gross sales of more than a billion dollars a year.

Harry Terrick, the manager of supply chain services at Regal, returned my call and said he could spare a few minutes to chat. A ruddy-faced man whose jowls suggested he'd earned the color from heavy drinking, not heavy exercise, Terrick sat at a modest desk inside his office. From his forced smile to rigid posture, he looked uncomfortable. Dark gray plastic valves and fittings were scattered on his desk between photos of his wife and grown daughters.

"On the phone you said you were an investigator and wanted to learn more about my dealings with Chan International. Are you with the police or some kind of agency?"

"No."

That seemed to relieve him for some reason, his shoulders dropping ever so slightly, and he settled back in his chair. He waited for me to add more to my answer. I did not accommodate him.

"Then why are you here?" he asked, breaking the uncomfortable silence in the office.

"I'm working on a matter for Granderson University, and Chan's name came up. You're listed on Chan's website, so I thought maybe you could tell me something about him."

"What do you want to know? I'll be upfront in telling you I can't divulge much, for proprietary reasons."

"I understand. Let's start with the basics. You're a client of Thomas Chan's company?"

"Yes, though we signed the contract only three or four weeks ago with the manufacturing firm Chan set us up with, so no work has actually started yet."

"If you don't mind my asking, what are you and Chan International working on together?"

"Chan is a go-between for US companies and Chinese companies, who can do certain jobs cheaper than we can here in the States, especially here in California. In our case, we have a new industrial valve line coming out at the end of the year. We wouldn't make a nickel on a single valve if we were to produce it here, so we're having the manufacturing done in China. It cuts our cost in half."

"Does Chan get a finder's fee for setting up the deal, or do they get a cut of all future manufacturing?" I had read an article a while ago on how manufacturer's reps work with offshore accounts and remember there were different payment models.

"In our case, a little of both, though I can't divulge the details. You know, I forgot about a meeting I have with my boss."

"I understand." Meeting with the boss. Forgot. Sure. Terrick's initial curiosity about an investigator contacting him had evaporated like a mud puddle in the desert.

"How long have you been working with Chan's firm?"

"Oh, gosh, about four or five months. It's been kind of an on-again, off-again process with them."

"How so?"

He glanced at his watch. "We thought we had a deal with the manufacturer three months ago. But there were some added fees we didn't understand."

"What kind of added fees?"

"I don't know. I really shouldn't talk about our business."

"It's just between you and me." I had wondered how Chan's firm had supposedly been so successful so quickly. Something in Terrick's manner gave me an inkling.

He sighed. "There was something called an inspection fee. About a hundred grand. A hundred grand's not a lot in the big picture, but we had questions about it. Next thing we know, the fee went away, and we went forward with the deal. I think Thomas did something to convince the company to drop it."

"What do you think that something was?"

Terrick shrugged and looked distractedly at something on the wall to his right.

"Do you think Thomas paid the fee?"

"How would I know? All I know is Regal no longer had to pay the fee." Terrick turned his head towards me, though he didn't meet my eyes.

"What about you?"

"What about me?"

"Was there anything in it for you?"

"What do you mean by that?"

"Did Chan give you any incentive to make the deal?"

His face reddened, either from embarrassment, anger, or both. He pressed his lips together so tightly they turned white.

"I'm not suggesting a bribe. I'm just wondering if—"

Before I could finish the sentence, Terrick moved around his desk and stood next to me. "I really do have to go. Please see yourself out." A moment later, he walked out of his own office, leaving me with my question hanging in the air.

An hour later, I arrived at SMUD. One of my students at Sacramento State during my days as a professor now ran the corporate communications department at SMUD. Roger Talbert and I drank coffee from the machine in the company cafeteria. Roger had been one of my favorite students. Bright and inquisitive, he wrote well, spoke like a pro, and possessed remarkable common sense for a college student. I knew he would be successful, and this was evidenced with his position at SMUD, where he ran a thirty-two person department responsible for all forms of public communication, from newsletters and videos to the website, brochures, speeches, and social media outreach. Not bad for someone a year or two north of thirty.

"I'm getting married later this year," he said after we'd settled down at a table. A handful of other employees sat at other tables, chatting on cell phones, reading, or just daydreaming during their coffee break.

"Congratulations! Do I know this woman?"

"Probably not. She works here."

I raised an eyebrow. "Oh."

"It's not what you think. She works in a different part of the company. We didn't even meet at work. We have mutual friends."

"If you say so."

"Now you're just messing with me."

"It's what I do best."

A cafeteria worker straightened chairs at some of the unoccupied tables. He then proceeded to vacuum the carpet at the far end of the room. It was nearing four o'clock, the end of the workday.

"So, professor, it's an honor to see you again and have coffee. But, somehow, I don't think you called to catch up socially."

"Am I that transparent?"

"Pretty much."

"I'm not sure if you know this, but I retired from Sac State and now have my own investigation business."

"I did hear that. Bunch of bullshit, excuse my French, about the sexual harassment thing. I'm sorry about that. Wasn't fair to you."

I raised my right palm to thank him and indicate further empathy wasn't needed. "It's done. And in the end, it turned out to be a good thing."

"Still, it wasn't right."

"No, but I'm over it." I took a sip of coffee, remarkably tasty for vending machine brew. "I did want to ask you a couple of questions, if you don't mind, about your working relationship with a company called Chan International."

"What about them?"

"Their website says you were a client, and they had brokered some printing services over in China for you."

"They did as a matter of fact. They won the contract for printing our marketing collateral—brochures, annual reports, bill inserts, that kind of stuff. It was a three-year contract worth about a million dollars. They came in about twenty percent lower than the next lowest bidder."

"Was the only selection criteria low price?"

"No, but it was about two-thirds of the equation. They seemed too low, so I was part of a review team to vet their proposal. They were partnering with a firm over in China to do all the printing. Chan was a go-between."

"When your team finished its evaluation, did the contract hold up?"

"Kind of, though we ran into one stumbling block. There was a fifty thousand dollar line item in the contract for a government inspection fee. Our legal department wanted to know what that was. Chan was evasive at first, then pretty much admitted it was a gift of goodwill, that's what he called it, to the printing company's family."

"Did you pay it?" The additional fee sounded a lot like what Terrick had encountered. I wondered if this was the standard operating procedure in China or just the firms Chan International dealt with.

"No, of course not. We're a public agency. Everything needs to be transparent. We told Chan the fee had to be dropped or we couldn't do the deal."

"And the fee went away."

"Yep."

"I'm going to ask you a question with all due respect, and only because it could be relevant in something else I'm working on. Did Chan offer you any incentives to take the deal?"

Roger turned his attention to the top of the table, where he spent several seconds turning his paper cup of coffee around and around. "I'll tell you this because I know I can trust you," he said, his eyes still cast down at the table. "He did suggest a kickback. I mean, not on the order of fifty thousand dollars, but he said he would give me season tickets to the Kings and a membership to the Sutter Club. I didn't take it, of course."

"But you didn't throw him out the door?"

"No," Roger said, looking me in the eyes. "To be honest, I didn't know how to do so without generating some bad publicity. Like I said, we're a public agency, so everything we do is open for Public Records Act requests. I figured declining the offer meant no harm, no foul. I guess I wussed out. I'm not proud of it."

ten

I ARRIVED AT GRANDERSON UNIVERSITY in plenty of time to meet Professor Kenneth Wiggin in his third-story office in Sieboldt Science Center. His door was opened a crack, so I knocked on the doorframe, stuck my head inside, and waited for him to look up from his desk. He was concentrating on his laptop, jabbing at his mouse pad with impressive zeal. I'd set up the meeting with the biology department's secretary and hoped Wiggin had checked his calendar after arriving late the night before from Germany.

"Professor Wiggin," I said when he did not turn around after a few seconds. He continued to busy himself with the laptop. "Professor Wiggin," I said louder.

"Come in, come in," he said, not looking at me. "No need to yell."

I entered and sat down. His office was unremarkable, except for the framed print on the wall behind him featuring a collage of marijuana leaves in varying shades of purple, red, yellow, orange, and green. The professor continued his fixation with the laptop. From his vitae, I put his age at about seventy-five. He looked twenty years younger than that, his hair a tangle of brown and gray curls, a droopy gray mustache his signature feature. "Damn!" he said, banging his palm down on his desk. "Thirty-four. Just missed it."

"Research project?" I asked, pointing at the laptop.

"Minesweeper. I missed the world record for expert level by one second. Damn!"

"There's always tomorrow."

"You're the private investigator my secretary told me about?" He raised his eyes from the computer screen to look at me.

"Ray Courage." I stood from the seat and reached across his desk to shake hands. "University security has asked me to look into the theft of your Monarch Project."

"I don't mean to be rude, but we're going to have to keep our meeting to fifteen minutes."

"Another game of Minesweeper on the calendar?"

"Nope. Just got booked for a meeting. Now what can I do for you?"

"How was your trip to Germany?" Start with niceties. Rule Two from the Ray Courage Manual.

"It sucked. Cold as hell over there. After five days of German food, I got a case of the runs. The damn Krauts at the university were a bunch of cold bastards. Waste of time, the whole trip."

"Then you come home to find your project is missing."

"Helluva week." He went back his computer, which I guessed meant he was making another run at the Minesweeper record. "Do you surf?"

"Excuse me?"

"Do you surf? You know, ride the waves. Skim the tide." He gave me a "hang lose" gesture with his right hand.

"I'm afraid I don't."

"I was at Mavericks out at Half Moon Bay last month. Gnarly stuff going down out there. Those dudes can ride. Too much for me, but I love watching 'em. Heading out to Maui next month to surf Jaws, though. That'll be awesome."

Totally.

"You don't seem concerned about the fact your project has gone missing," I said.

"Not true. But what can I do about it right now?"

"Do you have any idea who would've wanted to steal it?"

"There are at least a hundred different assholes around the world who would know enough about the kind of work we were doing to want to rip us off."

"Would you consider any of them suspects?"

"Yeah." He laughed. "They're all a bunch of cutthroats. I'd say half of them would steal it if they had the chance. That's why I kept the data and research limited on an obscure server, where a hacker would have a near impossible time finding it. Didn't think someone would walk in and steal the server. Insane."

"Then there's the matter of them removing the project data from Jack's and Candace's computers. How do you think that happened?"

"Hell if I know. My data went missing, too. Someone hacked into all of our accounts and took it in one swoop."

"You had a cloud backup that got hacked into, too."

"Yeah. I didn't want to put it out there, but Candace and Jack said we needed it. I was like, if you say so." His surfer dude act baffled me. He was not at all devastated as Candace Symington had predicted.

"Who had the ability to do that? To hack into your system?"

"Who knows? I talked with the head of IT, and he said there appeared to be some breach, but it's one of those deals where the hacker routed his way through multiple computers. Kazakhstan, Mongolia, Russia. He said they couldn't trace it. They're bringing in an IT security consultant. I'm not getting my hopes up they'll do much better than our own IT guys."

I'd planned on talking to IT security staff, though I guessed they'd tell me exactly what Wiggin relayed. The "how" of the crime—or the details of the technical breach—seemed less relevant than "who." The theft seemed to be well-executed, and I doubted any forensic trail would lead me to the perpetrators. Narrowing down the list of suspects might give me the best chance of finding out who did it.

"What about your colleague in Davis, Corey Truxel? Do you think he could have done it?"

"Hell no. I bet Candace or Jack gave you his name. They don't trust him, but Corey's an old friend. We were smoking weed together in the sixties before it became cool." He shook his head at some memory his statement had conjured. He hummed the first few bars to the Grateful Dead's *Truckin'*.

"What about Stone Creek Saviors? Did Candace show you the note from them?"

"Yeah, yeah. They might have done it. But nobody knows who the hell they are."

"Did they contact you?"

"Check this out," he said, turning his laptop around towards me. He pulled up a YouTube page and started a video of a guy riding a wave at least fifty feet high. "Mavericks from last year! Is that crazy or what?"

"So this note to Candace is the only contact from Stone Creek you've received?"

"Yes."

He continued watching the Mavericks video, turning the sound up so we could both hear the roar of a massive wave.

"Candace thought you'd be devastated over losing the project."

He smiled as he watched the video and then glanced over at me. "I'm not happy. But at my age, you've got to go with it. I still have a cool job and get paid the same either way. Besides, I think our corporate sponsors might want to pay the twenty million dollars."

He gave me another "hang loose" sign, my cue to exit the nineteen sixties and return to the twenty-first century.

eleven

I RAN INTO CANDACE SYMINGTON outside Professor Wiggin's door. Her face was drawn tight, and it appeared she might not have slept in some time.

"Hi," I said. "He's a bit busy right now. There's a Minesweeper record that needs breaking."

Despite her apparent stress, she uttered a token laugh. "So you met him."

"Is he always like that?"

"You mean a combination of ADD, too much LSD, and 'Don't Worry, Be Happy'?"

"Not what I expected."

"Are you going to the meeting?"

My blank expression gave her my answer.

"Our corporate investors called a meeting. They heard about Monarch. They're not very happy at the moment."

"When's the meeting?"

"Five minutes in the faculty conference room down the hall. If you can, you might want to make it." That must have been the meeting Wiggin referred to earlier.

"Sure."

She excused herself and went in to talk to her boss. They were a strange pair. Candace Symington, the epitome of uptight and straight-laced. Kenneth Wiggin, a cross between Jerry Garcia and Homer Simpson. It was hard for me to imagine them communicating without driving the other crazy, let alone running a multimillion-dollar research project.

The faculty conference room featured a large rectangular table with at least twenty chairs. A row of seats rested against three of the wood-paneled walls in the narrow room, while the fourth wall consisted of a floor-to-ceiling window providing a nice view of campus. The room felt more corporate than academic, a place where in the old days deals were made over cigars and brandy.

A man and a woman in business suits commanded one side of the table, the woman in her mid-forties, dressed in a beige jacket over a wide-collared navy blouse. She sat upright and confident, as if she had called the meeting. The man next to her looked a bit older, with stooped shoulders, a bad comb over, and a physique suggesting an expense account diet and an exercise regime comprised of watching golf on TV. A blue blazer groaned from his heft, the days long gone when it could be buttoned closed. He stole an occasional deferential glance at the woman, confirming their pecking order.

Across the table, two more suits hunkered down. The older man wore an expression of self-importance and imminent flatulence. Next to him, the thirty-something man's hair had been cut, gelled, and tousled into stylish disarray. I could have sworn his coat and tie had been modeled by Derek Jeter on the cover of *GQ* the month before.

All four of them toiled away on smartphones, checking e-mails, text messages, or just avoiding eye contact or chitchat with anyone else in the room. I chose one of the chairs against the wall. At various times, each of the four others in the room sneaked a glance at me. I waved and smiled each time, not once receiving even a smile or a sneer in return.

Wiggin, Cassidy, and Candace arrived a few minutes later. Before they could take their seats at the head of the table, the woman started in on them.

"This isn't going to do, Ken," she said. "How long have you known about the theft? Huh? Tell me."

"Do you want that in American time or German time?"

"Don't be funny."

"You need to answer her question, professor," said her colleague.

"Hold on, hold on, everybody," Candace said, raising her hand in an attempt to calm the rising emotions. She sat in a chair, as did Wiggin and Cassidy.

"And who is that?" asked one of the men across the table from the woman. He was pointing at me.

I was about to stand, take a bow, and introduce myself, when Candace spoke again. It appeared her pre-meeting with Wiggin had been to establish herself as the facilitator of this meeting. After my ten minutes with the man, I believed she was wise to do so.

"Let's start with introductions. I know we've all communicated the past few years by e-mail and by conference call, but this is the first time we've all been in the same room together. I'll start. As you know, I'm Candace Symington, one of the leads on Monarch. And Dr. Wiggin is, of course, the head of the project."

"Call me Ken," he said. Candace shot him a quick look.

"And I'm Jack Cassidy, lead engineer." Jack half stood and then settled back in his seat.

"Now let's go around the room and have you introduce yourselves," Candace said. "Let's start with you, Mr. Courage."

I introduced myself, and a buzz filled the room.

"An investigator?"

"What about police?"

"The feds!"

"Does he have a security clearance?"

"I'm not sure I like this."

And so on.

It was nice to be wanted.

"Please, everybody," Candace said, trying to regain control. "We'll explain where things stand, including Mr. Courage's role, in a minute, but let's continue with the introductions. Trudy." She nodded at the woman to her left.

"Trudy Nichols, director of private sector investment, Sunrise Oil Corporation." She struck me as an alpha type who ran marathons, ate vegan food, and didn't take flack from anybody. Sunrise Oil. Seth Seeger had known they were one of the investors in Wiggin's project. I pondered why an oil company would invest in a technology destined to eliminate the need for their product, deciding Sunrise probably wanted to grab the next big thing in energy and profit from it rather than have it bury their company.

The puffy guy next to her spoke next. "Dick McBright, chief financial officer, Sunrise Oil."

Across the table, an older man, pushing seventy, in a gray suit and red tie introduced himself. "Arnie Chipperfield, chief investment officer, North America Fuel Cell Corporation." He turned to look at the younger man to his right.

"Tyler Ball, investment analyst, NAFC." Ball, the youngest and lowest-ranked of the corporate representatives, seemed to be the most peeved. He reminded me of a petulant twelve year old in a too-big suit who might erupt any second into a foot-stomping tantrum.

"Very good then," Candace said. "What I'd like to do is recount, step by step, the events of the past three days, then talk about the plan going forward. I would like to respectfully ask you to allow me to finish before we go to questions and discussion."

Ball rolled his eyes at the idea, drawing a stern look from old Arnie.

Candace walked through the events starting three days ago with her ill-fated return to the lab soon after she had left for the day. She ended by holding up a copy of the note demanding the twenty million dollars in exchange for the project.

"Shouldn't the police have that?" Trudy asked.

"No," Candace said, shaking her head. "The note says if we go to the authorities the project will be gone forever."

"How would they ever know?" Dick asked.

"I don't know," Candace said. "You have a lot of money invested in Monarch. Do you want to take that chance? We want to get your input first before deciding what to do about the note. If the police get in the middle of things we could risk scaring off these 'Saviors' and losing the project for good."

"The question is," Wiggin said. "Do we want to spend twenty million dollars to retrieve the project?"

"You mean do *we*," Arnie said, pointing at his team and then at Trudy Nichols and Dick McBright across the table. "Sunrise and NAFC."

"Pretty much," Wiggin said with a chuckle. "Candace, Jack, and I don't have that kind of bread."

"What a fucking mess," Tyler said.

"What assurances do we have that even if we pay the twenty million dollars these people—whoever they are—will return the project intact?" Trudy asked. "Hell, they might not even have it."

"We have no assurances they'll return it or if they have it," Candace replied. "But we could ask for a show of good faith. Make them turn over part of the project—maybe some of the genome sequencing—to make sure they have it. But we can't guarantee they'll return it."

"I think the authorities should be brought in," Arnie said.

"I disagree," Trudy argued. "I think Candace is right on this one. We can't risk losing the project. We've got more than a hundred million dollars invested in it and NAFC has fifty million. We're seeing this as an investment that'll be worth billions to us in a few years, and I'm sure you do, too. Do you want to put that on the line? Would your board of directors?"

The meeting broke down after Candace's comments, the employees from the two companies breaking into their own sidebar conversations. Arnie Chipperfield pulled out his phone and stabbed at the keypad with his fingers.

"Please!" Candace said. "Everybody, please. Arnie, put down your phone. We need to decide what we're going to do here."

"Chill everybody!" Wiggin said.

The clamor subsided, Arnie returned his phone to his coat pocket, and Candace turned her attention to me. "What do you think, Mr. Courage? What do you think we should do? You're the expert when it comes to security and investigation."

"Or as close as we've got, which isn't saying much," Tyler said.

Prick. I gave him a withering stare, evoking a return smile. I needed to practice my withering stare in the mirror. I stood to address the group. "I should look into the S-SOP organization to see if I can shake anything out of them."

"Who's S-SOP?" Trudy asked.

"It's an eco-group on campus that's alleged to have resorted to terrorist tactics in the past. We think they could be behind this," I replied. "In the meantime, if you receive another note or other form of communication, I think we should play along with them, starting by asking them for proof they really have the project. Candace, I think your idea of asking for a piece of the project in advance is a good one."

"What about going to the police?" Arnie said.

"Or the FBI?" Tyler added.

"This would be an FBI matter. It's up to you, but at some point you have an obligation to tell them about the theft of Monarch and the note. Campus security also needs to know before you go to the feds."

Trudy looked worried when I said that. "You may be right," she said. "But can we all agree to wait until we hear back from these extremists? I, for one, would be willing to commit Sunrise to paying half the twenty million in exchange for the safe return of the project."

"I agree," said Dick.

After several seconds, Arnie gave a slight nod. "Okay, but only for a day or two. If we don't get Monarch back by then, we call the FBI."

"Trudy, you said Sunrise would be willing to pay ten million." Candace then turned to the NAFC side of the table. "Arnie, what about your company? Could you come up with ten?"

"I suppose," he said. "We're not a big oil company like my colleagues across the table. But we've budgeted for more research with Granderson this year. It will blow my budget, but if it gets the project back then it'll be worth it."

"All right, it's settled then," Candace said. "I'll let you all know when I hear back from these creeps, and we'll take it from there. Would video teleconference work? I know how hard it is for Sunrise to get here from the Bay Area."

Everyone nodded.

"Good. And one last thing, I would suggest limiting who you tell about this to those who absolutely need to know. We can't risk losing Monarch. We've got too much invested in it."

twelve

I OPENED A BOTTLE OF Rubicon IPA and poured it into a glass, the creamy, billowing head receding to reveal the amber red surface. I took a thirsty sip, and then another. While the gas grill heated up, I threaded cubes of sirloin, button mushrooms, and pieces of yellow bell pepper and red onion onto wood skewers. I had already prepared a Tandoori sauce I'd serve with the kebobs over rice. From the kitchen speakers connected to my iPod, Steely Dan belted out "Deacon Blues" from the *Aja* album. When the last track from the album played out, it segued into *Gaucho*, my favorite Steely Dan CD.

After dinner, I cleaned the dishes and put the leftover kebobs in the refrigerator for lunch the next day. About eight o'clock, I was contemplating a third beer and reflecting on the events of the day. Harry Terrick's and Roger Talbert's stories about their dealings with Chan nagged me. Had Chan and Benzer come up with a hundred and fifty thousand dollars to grease the palms of the Chinese? And who knew what they gave Terrick? It was a lot of money for two guys right out of grad school. And that was just for those two deals. How many more palms did they grease, on either the Chinese or US side of the equation?

Chan's relationship with Candace Symington and Chan's shady business tactics kept drawing me back to Chan International. Too much was going on there for it not to be connected to the Monarch theft.

I picked up my phone and called Chan International, hoping the call might forward to Chan's or Benzer's personal cells. It didn't. Chan's house was less than five miles from mine, and only two beers into the evening, I felt fine to drive.

When I pulled in front of his house, disappointment washed over me. The place was dark; not even a porch light had been turned on. Maybe he was reading, working, or watching television in a back room, the light not visible from the street. I walked to the porch and noticed the doorframe had been splintered, the door ajar. From inside the house, heavy metal music banged, so loud there on the porch it had to be intolerable inside, even for the most resolute metal head.

"Thomas?" I shouted, parting the door and sticking my head inside.

I shouted his name again, though he'd be hard-pressed to hear me over the din. My first instinct was to retreat and call the police. Then again, though I didn't like him, Thomas Chan could be in trouble and even a short delay while the police arrived might be disastrous. Or, on the other end of the spectrum, maybe he was having sex in his bedroom, the loud music his strange aphrodisiac. Calling the police might embarrass Chan, make me look stupid, and piss off the cops, broken doorframe or not.

Inside the darkened entryway, I ran my hand along the wall for a light switch. The first switch flicked on the porch light, the second the entryway. Everything in the living room and dining room looked undisturbed, just as it had appeared the day before.

Though the music would have masked the sound of my steps on the hardwood floor, I tiptoed to the kitchen. A full bottle of wine sat open on the counter, an unused glass beside it. Everything else was spotless, no dirty dishes or other signs the kitchen had been recently used.

"*Thomas!*" I called again. I picked up a flashlight on a small table in the utility area beyond the kitchen and turned back to explore the rest of the house. The flashlight needed batteries, but its weak beam provided enough light to enable me to locate the source of the music—a cell phone plugged into two speakers on the mantle. I turned the music down below earsplitting level, but loud enough to mask any sound I might make walking through the house.

The opened door to the first bedroom revealed it had been converted into an office. Sweeping the room with the flashlight confirmed it was empty and appeared to have been undisturbed. I worked my way down the hall to the next door, which opened into a bathroom. Again, nothing. At the end of the hall awaited two rooms, one to my left, the other to my right.

I checked out the room on the right first because its door was opened but found nothing more impressive than a standard bedroom with an undisturbed bed, a nightstand, and a dresser. That left what had to be the master bedroom. No light shone from underneath its door. I turned the doorknob enough to confirm it wasn't locked.

"Chan," I said in a voice just above the music in the other room. A few seconds later, I knocked and repeated his name. I put my ear to the door and heard nothing on the other side. Opening the door halfway, I looked through the opening and saw a figure lying on the bed. Again, I called his name. When he didn't answer, I shone my flashlight at the bed.

With its back to me in a fetal position was a fully-clothed man lying atop the bed. I switched on the overhead light. If the man noticed the light, he didn't react to it. He was wearing a white T-shirt and tan pants, with no shoes or socks. At the side of the bed I reached over and gave his shoulder a push and then stepped back. He didn't awaken. When I went to the other side of the bed, I could see no amount of pushing would rouse Thomas Chan.

The chocolate colored handle of a butcher knife protruded from his gut, the bedspread on his front side saturated with blood. Chan's eyes were wide open and, for a moment, I felt as if he was pleading for help, that I had not arrived too late. His right arm splayed out on the bedspread at a right angle to his body.

I gasped when I saw why he needed the bandage earlier in the day. The gauze had been unwrapped and lay in a pile on the floor.

The ring and index fingers of the hand had been cut off, the thumb and pinky folded down towards his palm, leaving his middle finger extended in an unmistakable "fuck you" gesture.

The sight unnerved me almost as much as Chan's bloody corpse. I stepped back and looked around the room. On the wall above the bed, scrawled in blood, were three letters: SCS.

thirteen

I DIDN'T SLEEP THAT NIGHT. The Sacramento Police Department kept me occupied until one in the morning with questioning, fingerprinting, and lab work to determine if any of Chan's blood had splashed onto my body when I knifed him. I tried to tell them about the Golden Dragon gangster I'd spotted earlier in the day, but they were more interested in my relationship to Chan. When I offered my opinion on the meaning of the SCS letters on the wall, I drew smirks from both detectives interviewing me. In the end, they released me, though they wouldn't declare me free and clear of the crime. I was asked not to leave the Sacramento area without letting them know.

At nine the next morning, I drove to the offices of Chan International, located on the corner of 20th and S streets, a midtown Sacramento mixture of craftsman homes and single story commercial buildings. Chan's office was housed in a flat-topped stucco structure divided into four quarters, each quarter home to a different business. I tried the glass door to the office, but it was locked. I hit speed dial on my cell.

"Hey," Rubia answered.

"Adam Benzer. MBA from Granderson. Works for Chan International. Can you get a home address for him?"

"Well, hello to you, too."

I gave a theatrical sigh. "Good morning, Rubia. How are you?"

"Better. What's the deal with Benzer?"

I told her what I remembered from his website bio to help her narrow the search. I then recounted the gruesome scene I'd found in Chan's bedroom.

"Shit. Sounds like the Dragons," she said.

"Maybe. Right now the leader in the clubhouse is the SCS. But there's too much going on with Chan and his company to ignore."

We ended the call, and I returned to my car. Not five minutes later, Rubia called me back.

"That was fast," I said.

"The guy's in the online white pages. You could have done it yourself."

"It must have been simple if I could do it myself."

"Exactly."

"Just give me the address."

Fifteen minutes later I arrived at Benzer's apartment complex in South Land Park. The place had seen better days, a rundown two-story building with peeling white paint and overgrown shrubs for landscaping. The Plaza Arms Apartment sign out front was missing several letters, requiring *Wheel of Fortune* acumen to puzzle out the name.

Benzer's unit was in the front of the building on the second floor. I knocked. Someone moved about on the inside, and the light coming through the peephole darkened. I waved at the peephole and smiled. The door remained closed.

"Adam," I said to the door. "My name's Ray Courage. I'm an investigator. I'd like to talk to you about Thomas Chan. Open the door please."

Downstairs, an older couple stood outside an apartment watching me. In the apartment next door to Benzer's drapes parted and then closed when I glanced in that direction.

"Adam."

A few seconds later he opened the door. "What do you want?"

"First of all, I want to offer my condolences. I'm sorry about Thomas's death." I didn't know the extent of the two young men's relationship. Even if they hadn't been friends, solely business partners, it had to be tough losing a colleague like that, especially one so young.

"You said you're investigating his murder. Do you have some ID?"

I gave him a business card. He frowned as he read it. People did that a lot with my card. Maybe I needed a new design.

"You're not a cop? I thought you said you were a cop."

"I said I was an investigator, not a cop. Can I come in?" The older couple continued to rubberneck us, and I didn't want them to overhear our entire conversation.

"What are you investigating?" He didn't seem to be too distraught about Chan's murder. His antsy manner suggested paranoia rather than sorrow.

"That's a good question." I was tired and didn't know what to say. The Monarch Project had been the initial object of my investigation; now it seemed to include Thomas Chan's murder. "It's a matter tangential to Thomas's death."

"Tangential? What the hell's that mean?"

"Can I come inside?"

After a pause, he stepped back and let me in. The inside of the apartment was much neater and more well-maintained than the apartment complex itself. Though the furnishings appeared to come straight out of an Ikea catalog, Benzer's place looked more upscale than the dwelling of a typical recent college graduate.

"Can we sit down?"

Benzer didn't appear comfortable with the prospect of a lengthy visit, but he pointed to the living room where we settled into a couple of matching leather chairs. He was a bit on the chubby side, with a thatch of dark hair and a day's worth of stubble. He sat upright in the chair while I affected a comfortable slouch to try relaxing him.

"Nice place," I said. "Not far from your office, grocery store, and a couple of restaurants nearby. Everything you need."

An orange and white tabby cat emerged from behind the couch and approached me, rubbing its cheek on my shin. I reached down and petted it.

"Nice cat. What's its name?"

"Can I ask why you're here?"

"Do you know Candace Symington?" The cat slid past my leg and then returned in the opposite direction, again rubbing its cheek on my shin.

"Sure. She is…was…Thomas's girlfriend. Or ex-girlfriend, I guess."

"Did you know anything about her work in the science lab at Granderson?"

"Not a clue. We weren't friends or anything. I knew her through Thomas. The three of us didn't hang out or anything. It was more like 'hi' and 'goodbye' when she stopped by the office."

"Did you ever hear her mention anything about a project called Monarch?"

"Nope."

"What about Thomas? Did he ever mention it?"

Benzer shook his head, his face now a mix of anger and boredom.

"Do you know Professor Wiggin or Jack Cassidy?"

"Heard the names. Candace mentioned them every once in a while."

"I thought you only said hi and goodbye to her?"

"Oh my god! Are you always this literal? Look, I just lost my friend and business partner. I don't need this bullshit. Please leave." He stood up and seemed to grow angrier when I didn't follow suit.

"Please sit down. I won't be much longer."

He still looked ticked off, but he sat down.

"Okay, so you don't know Wiggin or Cassidy."

"No, not at all."

"Can you tell me a bit about your business, Chan International? From what I've learned, your business model is to connect US companies with offshore manufacturers."

"I don't see why we need to discuss my business. I'm not sure what you're driving at here. You asked about Thomas's girlfriend and her work, and then you want to know about our business. What are you investigating?"

"It's complicated. Just help me understand a few things. From what Thomas told me yesterday, and what I gather from your website, you and Thomas brokered business deals between US companies and Chinese manufacturers."

"Yeah, that pretty much covers it. We have clients all around the country and some local ones, too."

"Like Regal Systems and SMUD."

"Yeah."

"You managed to put together pretty big deals for both of them. Not bad for a couple of guys recently out of business school."

He glowered at me. "You've been digging into our business with clients?"

"I talked to a couple of people."

"You *talked* to our clients? Goddamn it! You have no right to do anything like that."

"Take a valium there, Mr. Paranoid. I didn't do anything to compromise your business dealings."

He fumed, and I sensed he was about five seconds from showing me the door. I understood his not appreciating my talking to his clients. No businessman would. But his reaction seemed out of proportion to the offense.

"Can you tell me more about the inspection fees related to the Regal and SMUD contracts?"

"No." His jaw was so tight I thought he might grind the enamel off his molars.

"Harry Terrick and Roger Talbert said there were kickbacks to the Chinese companies. When they raised the issue with you, the inspection fees disappeared. How did that happen? Did the companies withdraw their demand for a kickback? Or did Chan International cover it so you wouldn't lose the deal?"

He shook his head in irritation. "American companies don't understand how business is done around the world. There are certain customs and operating procedures that need to be followed to get the best deal possible. The Chinese companies we partnered with for Regal and SMUD expect a relatively small cash gift as a show of good faith."

"Sounds like a bribe to me."

He shrugged. "It's not illegal. Look, these companies put in such low bids that their margins were minimal. They did so for two reasons. One, to keep their employees working. And two, to build relationships with US companies in the hopes of future business. The gifts are a goodwill gesture to the Chinese executives for selling their services at such a low price."

"So tell me, did they drop the request or did you pay it?"

"We paid it, okay! It's not a big deal. Now get out, please."

He stood, walked over to the door and opened it. I started to ask him about the bribes offered Terrick and Talbert, then thought better of it because it would shed no new light on where they'd gotten so much cash. As I reached the door, I stopped to face him.

"Where did you get that kind of money? A hundred and fifty thousand to pay off the Chinese? And that's just for two clients. How much more in kickbacks have you paid for other clients?"

"My parents loaned me the money, okay? Now get out of here."

"Well, I don't have to be told twice," I said. "Well, maybe I do. By my count that's the third time you've asked me to leave."

He did more of the jaw-clenching thing. I was an expert on personality types, but this guy was definitely a Type A, a heart attack waiting to happen in ten years, if not sooner.

"Have a nice day." I smiled at him as I stepped through the doorway.

He slammed the door. The older couple downstairs stared up at me. I smiled at them and headed for my car.

fourteen

I LOOKED AT THE BAG on the passenger seat, the stapled prescription form with my name, the drug name, and the dosage instructions. Zoloft. Active ingredient: Setraline, an antidepressant of the selective serotonin reuptake inhibitor class. I'd read about it before going to the pharmacy to pick up the prescription, which I'd let sit for three days. I wasn't much for meds. I stuck the unopened bag into my glove compartment. Since visiting Dr. Nelson, the nightmares had vanished, the images of bullet-riddled bodies no longer my sleep companions. It was as if hearing him say the problem was in my head—real but in my head—and not rooted in a physical affliction gave me permission to vanquish the nightmares. The day visions persisted, but with less frequency and diluted intensity. My thoughts drifted back to that evening now and again as I relived the eerie stillness following the gunshots, the smell of cordite heavy in the air, Rubia's shocked face, and then the first words to break the silence: "Holy shit, Ray." I should have been more straight up with the doctor, telling him the real reason why the nightmares and visions troubled me.

I opened the heavy wooden doors leading into the Sacramento Oaks Country Club lobby. It was after ten in the morning. This was my first visit to the exclusive club east of downtown. The club's proximity to the capitol building reputedly attracted scads of legislators and lobbyists. I surveyed the room to determine where the business offices might be. In front of me, beyond the foyer, was a dining room with dozens of tables and a bar. At mid-morning, twenty or so members feasted on late breakfasts or early lunches. Except for a table with two couples wearing tennis whites, everyone wore golf clothes of varying degrees of garishness.

To my immediate right, a hallway led towards the pro shop I'd noticed on my walk from the car. Several door lined the hallway, which I took to be the staff offices. On the right side of the dining area was the marked entrance to the men's locker room. A similar entrance to the women's locker room was beyond that.

I headed down the hall as a woman emerged from an office and greeted me.

"You must be Mr. Courage." She had a sincere smile, her eyes looking into mine.

"Ray." I shook her hand and returned her smile.

"How nice to meet you. I'm Jolene Gillingwater. And please call me Jolene."

She was attractive, maybe early forties, blond hair parted on one side, allowing her long bangs to sweep across her forehead. She wore a black sweater, unbuttoned, over a gray patterned dress. She looked dignified, and I could see what Danny Cashmore saw in her. I had gone back and forth about the wisdom of meeting her face to face. I decided the odds of her putting me together with Danny were rare, given our infrequent socializing. Besides, I was curious about this woman and wanted to learn more than what an employment background check would reveal.

"You're right on time," she said.

"You know what they say about punctuality."

She gave me a quizzical look. "What do they say about punctuality?"

"I'm sure they say something. They have something to say about everything."

She laughed. "Can I get you a cup of coffee or something stronger from the bar?"

The coffee sounded pretty good, but I wanted to get through this as quickly as possible. I felt awkward snooping in on my friend's potential fiancé under the pretext of wanting to join her country club.

"No, thank you. I'd just like to learn more about the club."

"You said on the phone you were looking to get back into playing golf," she said.

"Yes, it's been a while since I've played, and I'd like to start up again."

"Well, I think you'll like what you see."

We walked towards the dining room, and she explained the operating hours of the kitchen and bar, the chef's credentials, special event dates, and so on. As we crossed the room, several of the diners assessed me with their eyes. Sacramento Oaks was by no means the fanciest or snobbiest club in town. But they had their standards. From the reflexive scowls I appeared to be eliciting, I didn't seem to be meeting those standards.

She opened a glass door beyond the bar and led me outside to a swimming pool deck. On the other side of the deck were six empty tennis courts. I'd given country club attire my best shot—loafers, blue khaki pants, a black and red polo, and a light gray jacket, which I wouldn't need much longer on the beautiful February morning.

"What are you looking for in a club?"

"Oh, one with a good golf course and members who aren't too snobby."

She laughed. She had a nice laugh, spontaneous, making her blue eyes sparkle. "We have the former. I can't guarantee the latter."

"I didn't appear to pass the test when we walked through the dining room."

"Oh, that." She waved a hand back towards the diners. "Don't take it personally. You know how it is. Once you gain access to something, you want to put up a sign saying 'closed.' All of a sudden nobody else is good enough to join. I've seen it everywhere I've worked."

"Have you worked in the country club business long?"

"My entire adult life. Started as a waitress in college working at Los Altos Country Club in the bay area. Earned my degree in hospitality management, got promoted to bar manager, then hospitality manager. After that I took the same position at Pebble Beach." She'd probably recited her oral resume hundreds of times in interviews and to club members and new friends, but her enthusiasm and the sparkle in her eye made it seem like she was telling it for the first time.

"Impressive. Why didn't you stay at Pebble? Hard to beat the beauty of that place."

"Oh, long story. But the short answer is my career was stuck there. My boss and his boss were going to be there forever, and I had ambitions to manage my own club." There was no bitterness in her voice when she said this. She knew how the world worked and what it took to succeed in it.

"So you came here."

"Not right away. First I worked at Auburn Hills as food and beverage manager for a year before I applied to every GM position I could find in Northern California. A few months later I landed here. It's been six months now, and I love it."

"I can see why. It's a beautiful club."

We walked on in silence, the only sounds the *schick, schick, schick* of automatic sprinklers beyond the fence and the honking of several geese flying by. I felt comfortable and at peace in a way I hadn't felt in months. Was it the beautiful setting? Or was it Jolene who made me feel this way?

"Tell me, Ray, why all of a sudden do you want to take up golf again?" She took us around the pool towards a wrought iron gate at the far end of the deck.

"I'm recently retired and finding I have a lot of time on my hands." It was true. At least the recently retired part.

"Oh my, you're much too young to be retired." She gave me a light slap on the shoulder.

"You'd be surprised. I'm either younger than I look, or you're just flattering me for my membership fee."

"You're funny." She smiled at me, and I found myself smiling back at her in a way beyond simple politeness.

We exited the pool deck through the gate and took a right on the asphalt path winding past the cart shack to the pro shop. She wore low-heeled pumps and walked in them with a grace suggesting she might have been something of an athlete in her youth.

"What did you retire from?" she asked after a few minutes.

"College professor."

"So you're good looking and smart."

"Now I know you're just buttering me up."

"I am shameless."

We wandered through the pro shop, its walls lined with new golf club sets for sale, the main space crowded with racks of outfits, barrels containing drivers, fairway woods, and specialty wedges. Jolene said the shop was more as a service to the members than an actual money-maker, the sales volume too low, their prices unable to compete with superstores and online merchants.

"So what do people do here when they aren't playing golf?" I asked as we exited the pro shop.

"It depends. About a quarter of our membership is younger families. They use the pool and some of our recreation programs for kids. You know, things like tennis camp, golf lessons, and some social activities. Our members with grown kids or no kids take advantage of everything from tennis to bridge tournaments. There's a core group of men who play poker on Thursday nights. There's probably twenty or more guys, and a handful of older women, who just like to sit at the bar and drink."

"I guess that's a sport in and of itself."

She gave me a polite laugh. "Would you like to take a tour of the golf course?"

I would have said no, just a quick look at it would be fine, but all of a sudden I did want to tour the course, to spend more time with Jolene. "Sure."

She commandeered a golf cart from the shack, and we soon headed off to the course. No one was at the first tee, where she stopped. The green expanse in front of us was majestic, and I felt a mystic blissfulness wash over me. Until that moment, I hadn't realized how much I missed golf.

"Par four, four-hundred-ten yard, dogleg right, water to the right of the green, number five handicap. A tough starting hole. Not unusual for a Jack Nicklaus designed course."

"Are you remembering that from the brochure, or are you something of a golfer yourself?"

"Four years varsity at Cal State, Monterey Bay."

"Nice," I said. "I played four years at San Jose State."

"Go Spartans," she said, giving me a high five.

We arrived at the second hole, a par five she said was the easiest on the course. "This hole is more forgiving. Long hitters can get there in two. Overall, the course is a par seventy-two with a rating of seventy-four point seven and a slope of one forty-three."

"That's pretty tough. What do you shoot on it?"

"I don't play enough to score well."

I stared at her to draw an answer.

"You're too much," she said. "My best round is a seventy-four."

"That's from the ladies tees no doubt."

"Don't tell me you're one of those male chauvinists."

"Quite the contrary. I believe in equal pay for equal work for men and women. And I believe we should all tee off from the same tee markers."

She smiled. She had a beautiful smile, one with a bit of mischief in it. "A bit touchy on that, aren't you?"

It was my turn to laugh. "I've been beaten too many times by good women golfers with a forty-yard advantage. I guess I need to get over it."

We spent the next thirty minutes cruising from hole to hole. It was a great layout, set amid legacy oaks, towering green pines, native grasslands, and a meandering creek. The fairways were as smooth as the putting greens on the public courses I used to play. I hadn't come to join the club, but by the time we'd finished I was considering it.

The tour ended back where we started inside the clubhouse. The dining room had filled up, the golfers and tennis players now joined by men and women in business attire. Some of the inveterate drinkers Jolene referred to earlier had taken seats at the bar, and the beer, wine, and martinis were starting to flow.

"What do you think of the club?"

"I like it," I said. "What does it take to join?"

"Twenty-five thousand to join with an equity share. Dues are two-forty a month—that includes unlimited golf—with a food and beverage minimum of sixty dollars a month. You can also choose to spend the sixty in the pro shop if you want."

I nodded and thought about the looks I'd attracted in the dining room earlier. "Is there some approval process, club tribunal, or initiation rites?"

"Yes. Our board of directors will interview you to determine your moral compass. Then, if they give the thumbs up, you'll pass through a gauntlet of all our members who will swat you on the butt with ping pong paddles." Her face looked dead serious.

"Really?"

She cracked a smile.

"Is any of that true?"

"Well, the board does need to approve all new members, but if you're not a practicing felon then that's a formality. The paddling part? Only if you want to."

"Let me think about it," I said.

"Getting paddled or joining the club?"

"Both."

We shook hands and, as we did, she reached out and touched my shoulder with her left hand. An awkward silence followed.

"I should get going. Thank you for the tour and the delightful morning. I'll get back to you in a couple of days." I headed for the front door.

"Ray," she said, and I turned back to face her. She took two steps towards me. "I hope you don't think this is unprofessional of me. I don't usually do this. But would you like to have lunch sometime?"

"You mean here at the club?"

"No. I mean socially, somewhere *not* at the club."

fifteen

IT TOOK AN HOUR THROUGH traffic to get to Granderson. After my meeting with Seth Seeger, I had searched the web for someone named Forrester. What I thought would be a needle in a haystack turned out to be quite easy, or at least I guessed as much. Granderson University had a Riley Forrester on its payroll, a tenured professor of sociology.

He'd published papers in several sociology journals. The titles of a couple of papers jumped out at me: "Eco-terrorism or Justified Resistance" and "Eco-terrorism? A Critical Analysis of Government Attacks on Environmental Activism."

The abstract on the first article described Forrester's paper as rejecting the notion all "ecotage" acts were acts of terror and considering them as warranted acts of civil disobedience. The second article was described as exploring the history of the so-called "eco-terror" movement and why the label was misplaced.

His name also turned up in a twenty-year-old news item from the *Humboldt Beacon*. As a graduate student at Humboldt State University, a couple hundred miles north of Sacramento, Forrester had been arrested for chaining himself to a giant redwood tree. His goal was to prevent a developer from cutting down dozens of redwoods to build a housing development.

I didn't find anything linking Forrester to the Stone Creek Saviors, though I found a short article in Wikipedia interesting:

> *The Stone Creek Saviors is a purported radical environmental advocacy group in Northern California. The group took credit for a 2004 bombing*

of a dam construction site on Stone Creek in Placer County, California. The dam was being built to divert water to a housing development. A subsequent letter to The Placer Herald *newspaper from an individual or group calling itself the Stone Creek Saviors claimed responsibility for the bombing. The group's aim was "to stop the raping and desecration of the land." To date, there are no known members of the group, though rumors circulate they have committed other eco-terrorist acts in California but have not claimed credit for them.*

As I made my way to the Social Science Building, home of the sociology department, I thought about my morning with Jolene Gillingwater. If she had not been dating Danny Cashmore, I would have jumped at the chance to have lunch with her. But if she was dating Danny, why did she ask me to lunch? Did she and Danny have different perceptions about their relationship? Was Danny mistaken about her feelings for him? Or did Jolene lack romantic feelings for Danny? Or was she the kind of woman who liked to date more than one man at a time? In the awkwardness following her lunch invitation, I entered her number into my cell phone, told her I'd check my calendar and get back to her. I figured after a few days Jolene would forget about me.

Forrester's office was locked, and no light appeared underneath the door. The sociology department secretary said she hadn't seen him but guessed he might be at one of his favorite haunts, the organic farm co-op on the eastern edge of campus.

I arrived at the farm where two women were pulling weeds between rows of knee-high plants. Beyond them a thin man in a gray T-shirt and battered blue jeans worked at a huge compost pile with a pitchfork. The two women and I exchanged smiles as I passed.

"What can I do for you?" the man asked as I approached, his back to me.

"Riley Forrester?"

"Yeah." He was lifting up big forkfuls of debris and turning them over.

"Do you have a second to talk?"

"Who are you?" He had yet to even glance my way.

"My name's Ray Courage. I'm an investigator. The university hired me to look into an incident over at Sieboldt."

He drove the pitchfork deep into the compost, gathering a large mass of the matter, then tossed it back to the center of the pile. He stuck the pitchfork into the ground, wiped his brow on the sleeve of his T-shirt, and turned to face me. He was medium height and build, with a full black beard he didn't bother to trim. Though not physically imposing, he had an unnerving intensity about him, his dark brown eyes penetrating me with suspicion and contempt. "What kind of incident?"

"I'm not at liberty to say. I'm not trying to be coy. Just following orders."

"Figures. Everything at this university appears to be shrouded in secrecy. Wouldn't be surprised if the administration worked for the CIA."

"I was wondering if you heard anything about what happened at Sieboldt."

"You mean the 'incident' you or anybody else can't talk about? Now how would I be able to know anything like that?"

"Rumors. Talk among your colleagues at the university. That kind of thing. I used to work at a university and know college professors are the biggest gossips on the planet."

"I don't have any colleagues at the university. Bunch of right-wing robots."

"I take it you don't share their ideology."

"You take it correctly." He struck me as a man who liked to use his words sparingly, preferring fragments to full sentences, grunts to actual words.

"Then why'd you take the gig?"

"I ask myself that every day. Short answer is because I was told when they hired me they wanted to diversify the politics on campus. So far, that diversity consists of me. And it's been five years."

One of the women came over. She had mousey brown hair parted in the middle and a freckled face. "We finished weeding, Riley. What do you want us to do next?"

He looked over to his right towards a small house, where a variety of other plants grew in various stages of maturation. "I noticed some snails by the spinach. Can you and Liz find and relocate them?"

The woman turned to take on her task.

"What can you tell me about S-SOP?" I asked.

"Student-run organization focused on environmental education."

"What about the Stone Creek Saviors?"

He looked at me for a few seconds, and I could practically see the wheels turning in his head. He reached over to take the pitchfork into his hands again and began working the pile anew. "Mythical organization. Created by the FBI to demonize all environmentalists. The very same people who first identified global warming."

"Al Gore?"

Forrester didn't have much of a sense of humor. Or maybe it was just me he didn't find funny. "No, not Al Gore. I'm talking about Earth First! And all the other organizations championing environmental causes since the sixties."

"You said the Stone Creek Saviors were mythical. You mean they don't exist?"

He picked up and heaved two forkfuls of organic matter in the pile before he answered. "That's right. Has anyone ever identified himself as a member? Has the FBI ever identified anyone?"

"Doesn't mean they're mythical," I said. "Just secretive."

"Would you say ghosts, goblins, and Big Foot are secretive? Or mythical?"

"Point taken. But at the Food Science building firebombing last spring, someone had spray-painted a big 'SCS' on the wall." I was speaking again to his back as he labored on. "The police thought that meant the Saviors were taking credit for the attack."

"Speculation."

"There's also speculation you're a member of the Saviors. Maybe even their leader." It was a wild-assed guess designed to move the frustrating conversation along.

He stopped working on the pile and pivoted, the pitchfork at his waist, its tines pointed at me. "Who told you that?"

"Secret." I kept my eye on the pitchfork and took a step back.

"That's bullshit. And it's slanderous. If I find out who's saying those things, I'll sue them for it."

"Why would you consider that slander? From your writings, I thought ecotage was a justifiable form of civil disobedience? If that's what the Saviors are doing, then by your standards it shouldn't be considered against the law. In that case it wouldn't be slander."

"Are you going to play word games with me? I'm busy here."

"Do you mind putting the pitchfork down? It's loaded and pointed right at me."

He lowered the tool.

"Did you have anything to do with the firebombing last spring?"

"We're done here," he said.

"Did you sabotage the research work of a certain professor over in Sieboldt a few days ago?"

"We're done!" He threw the pitchfork onto the compost heap and stormed off towards the nearby house.

"What about Thomas Chan?" I shouted.

If he heard me, he gave no sign of it as he marched on. A moment later, I heard the loud slam of a door.

sixteen

As I drove to Davis, I dialed Rubia again and spoke to her on the car's hands-free.

"'S'up, professor?"

"I've got some work for you. Actual paying work."

"*Aye chi mama.* I *thought* I saw a pig flying earlier today."

"Very funny."

"So what's up on the gig?"

I updated her on my visit to Sacramento Oaks and my conversation with Jolene Gillingwater, skipping the parts where she flirted with me and asked me out. I then told Rubia to check into Jolene's background, specifically to verify the work history she'd provided—Los Altos Country Club, Pebble Beach, and Auburn Hills—and whether she'd graduated from Cal State Monterey Bay.

"You want prior marriages, credit scores, property ownership, memberships, and all that, too?"

"Yeah, why not?" I sighed.

"Ray, do you have the hots for this chick or something?"

"No, why would you say that?"

"Raaaaay." She drew out my name for several seconds.

"No. She's dating a friend of mine, remember?"

"But you have the hots for her. I can tell."

I didn't say anything, the road noise filling the silence. How the hell could she tell?

"I think it's cute when an old guy like you likes a girl." She then sang a rap version of the old seventies song "Love Is in the Air."

"Did you step on a cat?"

"You don't know art when you hear it."

"Apparently. Now when can you get me the info on her?"

She promised to provide it to me within a few of days. I hoped she'd find some dirt on Jolene. That would make things easier. First, it would help me get over the sudden attraction I'd felt for her. Second, it might dissuade Danny from marrying her and thereby eliminating any future awkwardness—on so many different levels—if Jolene, Danny, and I were ever in the same room together.

Before I hung up I asked, "What have you found out about the Golden Dragons?"

"Still looking. But one of my contacts says they have a small cell here in Sacramento, two, maybe three gang members. Mainly, they're checking things out, seeing if it's worth it to set up shop. My guy doesn't think they've done much yet. They'd need more than a couple of guys to start any serious shit."

"What about the license plate?"

"Oh, yeah, the car's tagged to a dude named Wu Wing. Don't know jack about him yet. My LA guy's asking around."

"Okay. Could you try to find out if one of their MOs is cutting the fingers off their victims?"

"Ouch."

"And one more thing—"

"Is this a paid gig, too, because you're piling on, professor?"

"Yeah, yeah, quit crying. Can you find out who Adam Benzer's parents are and whether or not they have money?"

Corey Truxel's company was on the south side of Interstate 80 in a Davis industrial complex three blocks from the freeway. Though I had come unannounced, he seemed undisturbed by my visit. Like Wiggin, he looked to be younger than his seventy-something years. Short and of slight build, he had rosy cheeks and wavy blond locks showing no hints of gray.

"Ken said I might be getting a visit from you." He smiled, eyes beaming through round wire-rimmed glasses.

"Professor Wiggin is, ah, insightful."

Truxel laughed. "People misunderstand and underestimate him because of his personality, but the man is brilliant. I've always known that."

The small space looked like a cross between a science lab and a metal shop. Microscopes, electronic instruments, Bunsen burners, glass beakers of varying sizes, and other chemistry lab staples mixed with acetylene tanks and torches, power tools, and a floor-to-ceiling rack loaded with sheet metal, steel rods, and angle iron. Four men in lab coats worked at separate tables on a variety of equipment I didn't recognize. I knew from its one-page website Truxel Laboratories conducted research and development of microbial fuel cells and Corey Truxel earned a PhD from Berkeley in electrical engineering.

"What do you do here?" I asked as I surveyed the room.

"Do you want the long answer or the short one?"

"Short will do."

"We do R and D to improve the efficiencies of various types of microbe-powered fuel cells. Most of our work is done for engineering firms, energy companies, and a couple of auto manufacturers."

"So the work is similar to what Wiggin's team is doing over at Granderson?"

"In a sense, yes, though they're doing more genome sequencing than we do here. We do more testing of existing technologies with an eye towards improving their efficiencies. Dr. Wiggin is seeking to create new technologies."

We moved through the lab, Truxel pointing out to me here and there the projects they were working on at the tables we passed. He displayed a true passion for his work with the enthusiasm in his voice and the animated gestures he made as he pointed out aspects of each project. Most of it went right over my head.

"Are these all your employees?"

"Yes, just the five of us. We may be small, but we can outwork firms five times our size."

"Did Wiggin tell you anything about what happened at his on-campus lab?" I asked.

"Not in any detail, only that someone sabotaged his project. It sounded dreadful."

"Any idea who would do such a thing?"

"None." A one-word answer.

From my days working on the Sacramento State campus, I'd rubbed elbows with the school's science and engineering professors. Though I knew better than to generalize about any group of people, I felt assured in characterizing them as straightforward and guileless, their zeal for finding answers and solving problems so consuming it left little room for trickery or deceit. Truxel struck me much the same way. He could have been a class-one liar, but from the way he looked me in the eye with that one-word answer, it made me believe him.

"From what you know of Wiggin's work, do you think it would be worth a lot of money? By that I mean commercially, to an energy company or something similar?"

"Absolutely, Ken's characterization of their work made me believe it would be a major breakthrough in utility scale power production."

"Would it be something of interest to you?"

He laughed. "It would be of interest to anybody in the field of fuel cell technology. Hey, wait, what are you implying?"

"Just asking is all. I'm trying to find out who stole their project. And the only place I can figure to start is by, one, finding out who knew about what he was doing and, two, determining if they had sufficient knowledge and skills to do something with the project once they took it. So far that's proven to be a pretty short list."

"And I'm one of the people on that list."

"Nothing personal."

"Well, it is personal! You're accusing me of being a thief! And besides, your logic is flawed. It could be someone who had a vendetta against one or more people on their research team."

"Or some environmental wackos like Stone Creek Saviors?"

"Exactly. Those are the kind of people you should be looking at instead of insulting the likes of me."

Our exchange had led us nowhere. The Saviors or S-SOP might have had the desire to destroy anything they saw as anti-environment. Especially if they mistook Monarch as a fracking project as Seth Seeger had said. But the desire to steal Monarch was one thing. The capability to do so was something else.

As I mulled this over and waited for the heated air between Truxel and me to cool, my cell phone vibrated in my pocket. I retrieved it and looked at the text message from Candace Symington: *Ransom instructions just came in! Can you come to Sieboldt right away?*

seventeen

KEN WIGGIN, CANDACE SYMINGTON, and I sat in the faculty conference room in Sieboldt Science Center just before nine at night. A large high-definition video monitor had descended from the ceiling, obscuring the whiteboard behind it. The three of us sat at the conference table in seats nearest the blank monitor; a squat cylindrical camera the size of a large coffee cup had been positioned on the table in front of us.

Candace showed me the e-mail she, Cassidy, and Wiggin had received simultaneously. Its message had been brief:

> *You will pay us the $20 million in CASH, one-third in one hundred dollar bills, one-third in fifty dollar bills, and one-third in twenty dollar bills. This will weigh about one thousand pounds. One of you will rent a white minivan and drive to Corti Brothers Market next Tuesday at 6 pm with the money in mailbags inside the van. In the wine department, there is a rack displaying Talbot Bordeaux 1996. Take the bottle at the bottom of the wine rack. You will find a note taped to the bottom of the bottle with instructions. Follow them. If we see any cops or more than one of you driving the van, we will destroy Monarch.*
>
> *SCS*

It had arrived minutes before Candace texted me. While the timing of its arrival didn't altogether rule out Corey Truxel or one of his employees, it did appear unlikely one of them had sent the new ransom instructions while I was standing in their lab.

"So, Sunrise and NAFC know about the instructions?" I asked.

"No," Wiggin said. "I figured it best to tell everyone all at once. You know, like ripping a bandage off." To illustrate the point, he tore a phantom bandage from his arm.

At two minutes before nine, Candace used a remote to turn on the monitor. She then pointed the remote at the camera to activate it. Seconds later, the three of us appeared in the monitor's lower right quadrant, our images a bit distorted by the camera's wide angle lens.

"The others should be logging in any minute now," she said.

"Okay," Wiggin said. "I'll take the lead on our end."

Candace started to speak but then stopped herself.

"If this goes well, the conversation shouldn't take long," he continued.

I was feeling uneasy about the ransom plan. The extortionists held all the cards. Part of me wanted to turn the whole matter over to the FBI. Monarch had been missing for four days. If the ransom payment didn't yield the project, then there would be no choice but to bring in the feds. They wouldn't be pleased to learn it'd taken several days before we'd done so. I wondered if we might even be charged with obstruction or some other crime.

"Before they come on the line, I want to be clear about something," I said. "If this ransom drop goes south at any point we need to report it to campus security. And then get the FBI involved."

"Yeah, yeah." He gave me a backwards flip of his hand.

Less than a minute later, Arnie Chipperfield's image appeared in the upper left corner of the monitor. He looked to be seated at his desk, wearing a light blue dress shirt and a red tie with blue stripes. A few seconds later, Trudy Nichols popped onto the screen's upper right corner. She looked tired and a bit cranky, our conference call well-past normal workday hours, even for a hard-charging executive.

Wiggin greeted everyone. As he did, Candace used the remote to arrange the images on the corner so they were aligned from left to right—Arnie, Trudy, and the three of us in the conference room.

"We received the ransom instructions from SCS."

"What do they say?" Trudy asked, her voice eager, the possibility of Monarch's return giving her a shot of energy. Her sidekick from the other day, Dick McBright, was notably absent, Trudy apparently taking the reins for Sunrise on this operation.

Candace read the instructions from the SCS e-mail she'd printed out.

"I don't like this," Arnie said.

"I tend to agree with Arnie," Trudy said, her initial hopefulness fading. "Driving around town with that much money. It seems like we're setting someone up to get killed and lose all our money."

The three of us exchanged glances. "Please, I know it's not the most comforting process," Wiggin said. "But look at it as a positive, as a step to getting Monarch back."

"Did you get some assurances these people even have Monarch?" Arnie asked.

"Yes," said Candace. "I replied to the e-mail I read you and asked for the sequencing on one of the bacteria I'd done. They sent it back. They couldn't have done so unless they had the project in hand."

"I saw the e-mail," Wiggin said. "She's right."

A few seconds of silence ensued as everyone took in the implications of that. The extortionists appeared legit. The question was whether they could be trusted to return the project after they'd received payment.

"What kind of strategy options do we have?" Arnie asked, his voice still tinged with anger.

"The way I see it, it's not complicated," I said. "We can go one of two ways. Pay the money and hope for the best. Or get the FBI involved right away and oversee the drop. So, what will it be?"

Neither of our two callers spoke. They looked to be thinking and fuming.

"Shit." Trudy slumped back in her chair. "We can't risk losing it. If these Saviors find out the cops are involved, we're screwed. Even if they don't, but the cops fuck up, then we're still screwed." She said nothing for several seconds as she looked away from the camera. "They don't teach you how to handle situations like this in business school." She seemed to be talking to herself. "All right."

"So we're agreed to go through with paying the ransom tomorrow?" I asked. On the screen I could see four nodding heads.

"Why the hell do they want cash?" Arnie asked. "Like they said, it'll weigh half a ton."

"Setting up untraceable wire transfers is not as easy as it used to be," I said. "You can't do it sitting at your computer. It takes a while, and you have to put in fifty thousand or more to open it up. Unwieldy as that much cash is, it's probably easier for them overall."

"I might get fired over this," Trudy said. "It's going to be a great conversation going into the CEO's office in the morning asking for ten million in cash."

"He'll understand," Wiggin said. "He knows the value of our work."

Trudy's withering look seemed to have no effect on Wiggin. Had it been directed at me, I might have started crying.

For the next fifteen minutes, we talked about the logistics of collecting the cash and all the steps needed to deliver the extortion money. Tuesday was four days away. Four days, including a Saturday and a Sunday, to gather twenty million in cash. Not much time. But Trudy and Arnie agreed they could get it done. That left one order of business. Who would deliver the money?

To my surprise the choice had been unanimous: me.

eighteen

AFTER BREAKFAST THE NEXT TUESDAY, Rubia dropped me off at the Enterprise Rent-A-Car office on 16th Street, where I rented a minivan as instructed in the e-mail. From there I drove straight to Sunrise Oil's corporate headquarters in San Ramon an hour and a half away. The guard at the security kiosk directed me to a loading dock, where Trudy Nichols and I watched two workers hoist fifteen mailbags of cash into the back of the van. Trudy and I didn't exchange pleasantries. On the return trip, I stopped in Fairfield and bought five matchbook-sized GPS trackers.

I drove back to Sacramento and on to Rancho Cordova, a nearby suburb, where I repeated the loading exercise at the North American Fuel Cell's office, adding nine more mailbags to the collection. The back of the van sagged noticeably, but it drove fine as I returned home to wait out the two hours with a wine bottle at Corti Brothers until my designated meeting.

In the corner of my bedroom closet, I picked up and set aside my half-full laundry hamper, which sat atop a small gun vault. Lifting the vault, I carried it to my dresser. I entered the lock combination, opened the vault, removed the Glock 32 pistol, and loaded it with a full thirteen rounds of .357 bullets. For good measure, I stuck another magazine with thirteen more rounds in my front pocket.

I strapped the leather holster to my belt and inserted the gun so it rode at the small of my back where I could conceal it under a coat. I told myself I wouldn't need to use the gun. I hadn't entered the field of investigation to become some cowboy. I wanted to help people not hurt them. On the other hand, experience taught me non-violence wasn't always the most practical route to travel.

My life had changed so much since I'd retired from teaching college. When I thought about what I'd already done today—loading twenty million dollars of cash into a rented minivan—I shook my head. I'd moved from a world of theory, abstraction, and ideas into one of action, reaction, and cold reality. Before, I armed myself through scholarly research. Now, I armed myself with a gun. I might have told myself two years ago, hell, even a year ago, that my former life held superiority over one favoring the physical over the intellectual. I wasn't so sure anymore. There was something to be said for living in the reality of the moment, where there wasn't time to overthink or overanalyze, where stopping to ponder might get you in trouble, hurt, or even killed.

It was a quarter to six. Time to head out.

I entered Corti Brothers at six sharp and soon found the rack containing ten bottles of Talbot Bordeaux. I'd been anxious someone might've inadvertently purchased the bottle with the note until I saw the price tag affixed to the display bottle. The Talbot went for a hundred and fifty bucks each, making it unlikely they'd sell ten bottles after we received the ransom instructions.

I pulled out the bottom bottle and found the small scrap of paper taped to it. The message was created using words cut from a magazine and taped to the note:

Go to Effie Yeaw. Note taped to garbage can.

Effie Yeaw Nature Center at Ancil Hoffman Park out in Carmichael. My wife and I had taken our daughter Sara there a few times when she was a little girl. I wondered why they'd chosen this location for the drop. It occurred to me the long road leading from the park's entrance stretched across a small valley easily observed from the overlooking ridges. Someone could watch my progress from the entrance to the nature center. The nature center itself wouldn't be open at this hour, its parking lot likely empty and out of view from the main road. I wondered if there really was a note on the garbage can or if they would just steal the van and its valuable contents. I had hoped for the latter because I'd mounted a GPS tracker to the bottom of the van. The other four trackers I put in different mailbags, carving out space in four stacks of currency to hide them in the wrapped bundles.

The drive from Corti Brothers to Effie Yeaw took about fifteen minutes. The unlit country road from the entrance of the park to the center took me past the park's picnic grounds, golf course, and hiking areas. Lights from the expensive homes on the ridge above offered little illumination as I drove along at twenty miles per hour. Since leaving Corti, I grew edgier by the minute, unsure how this endgame would play out.

The nature center was dark and abandoned, no other cars in sight. I parked in front and, keeping the headlights on, got out of the van. I went to the only garbage can in sight, a few feet away from the center's front door. There was no note. I looked inside the can, but it had been emptied and a fresh plastic liner put in place, probably by the last employee closing down the center to prevent raccoons or other animals from making a mess. The can sat atop a four-legged iron stand elevating it above ground about four inches. The headlights provided enough light to confirm nothing alive lurked under there, so I reached in with my hand and felt underneath. My fingers detected something thicker than a piece of paper stuck to the underside of the stand, and I managed to yank it out.

The swatch of cardboard had been ripped from a box and contained more of the magazine words.

Sand Cove Beach Park.
Leave van. Put keys under van.
Walk to Virgin Sturgeon for next instruction.
Remember: we're watching.

We're watching. I had no doubt about that. I could all but feel the eyes on me as I stood, note in hand, bathed in the lights from the van.

I didn't know Sand Cove Beach Park, but I knew where the Virgin Sturgeon Restaurant was on the banks of the Sacramento River a few miles north of downtown. I pulled up the map program on my phone and found the location of Sand Cove, about a mile up river from the Virgin Sturgeon.

My cell phone rang when I merged onto Highway 50 towards Interstate 5. I answered warily, though I doubted my adversaries had my cell phone number or knew I'd been selected courier of the twenty million.

"Ray? It's Ken Wiggin. How are things going?"

"I don't know. I'm driving all over town at the moment. I think my next stop is where they're going to take the money, but I can't be sure."

"Where are you going?"

I paused. Our extortionists may not have known I was driving the van. Then again, maybe they did. And if so, there was a remote chance they could monitor my phone. They wouldn't like me telling someone else where I was delivering their twenty million. "Sorry, I can't tell you."

"Why?"

"I'll explain later."

"Have you seen anybody yet?" Wiggin seemed nervous, not the laid-back surfer dude I'd come to know.

"No, not so far." I checked the rearview and side mirrors on the van. "I'm not sure if I will."

"Be careful. This is some scary shit. When it's over, call me back."

"You'll be my first call."

I took I-5 through downtown and exited on Garden Highway, which bordered the east side of the river. Once I passed the Virgin Sturgeon, I slowed to thirty miles an hour, unsure how well marked the entrance to Sand Cove would be. Garden Highway was a narrow two-lane road with no street lighting and light traffic this time of evening.

The phone rang again as I located the beach park's entrance.

"Is everything okay?" Candace asked when I answered.

"Smooth as can be." My voice was shallow, unable to mask my nerves. I turned left onto the entry road to the park.

"Where are you?"

"About to make the drop, I think."

"Mr. Courage, do what they say. It's not worth you getting hurt. Not even for twenty million dollars."

"Thanks. I'll remember that."

"I mean it," she said and hung up.

The van crept along at less than ten miles an hour as I tried to determine if anyone else was in the area. The road made a one-eighty degree loop and opened onto a rectangular parking lot behind a thicket of trees about a hundred yards from the highway. The lot was large, enough spaces for forty or fifty cars. It was empty now. I made a lap around the lot, which was surrounded by trees on all sides, the river about fifty feet away to the east.

I left the van parked in one of the spaces at the far end of the lot, tossed the keys on the ground under the driver's side door, and began the hike towards the Virgin Sturgeon.

nineteen

ONCE I HIT GARDEN HIGHWAY, I took a deep breath, the tension in my shoulders easing. If someone wanted to take me down, their best shot would've been in the parking lot by the river. I patted the gun on my back for comfort and continued up the dark road. The night had turned cold, my breaths billowing into clouds as I walked, hands thrust in my front pockets for warmth. About fifteen minutes later, I arrived at the restaurant.

The original Virgin Sturgeon had actually been on a barge floating on the river. It sank about forty years ago and was replaced by the current structure, which cantilevered off the roadside levy and hung over the riverbank. The descent from the road to the restaurant ended with a thirty-foot tunnel made of corrugated sheet metal that deposited you at the hostess station. The place was river rustic, the kind of restaurant you'd find on Guy Fieri's *Diners, Drive Ins and Dives*. All of the fifteen or so tables were occupied, and the bar was packed. I managed to find a barstool at the far end of the bar. The banter and laughter filling the room seemed strange, normal sounds of good cheer oblivious to my mission as a courier of twenty million dollars to an unseen criminal. Rather than calm or reassure me, the noise in the room put me more on edge. I told myself to take deep breaths of air.

My hands shook as I tried to retrieve my cell phone. The note had said to walk to the restaurant for my next instructions. But how was I going to get instructions here? Was someone in the crowd of drinkers and diners in on the conspiracy? Was one of them observing me as I sat at the bar?

I pulled up the map on my phone. The GPS tracker under the car showed it was still positioned at Sand Cove. Same thing with the other four GPS trackers I had inserted into the packets of money. So far, the van hadn't been moved.

We're watching. That's what the note said. As much as I had the sense of being watched at Effie Yeaw, I felt it a hundred times more so at the bar. I looked around the room. No one seemed to be looking at me. At the same time, I felt everyone was sneaking peeks when I looked away. Two windows flanked the liquor rack in the center of the bar. The inside light reflected off their darkness, and I could get a decent look at everyone sitting at the bar. We were an eclectic mix, young and old, men and women, black, white, Asian, and Hispanic. No one looked out of place. Then again, I hadn't any notion whatsoever of who to be looking for.

My heart beat hard against my chest. When I scanned the room yet again, everything seemed surreal, as if I were watching a movie of the scene rather than being a part of it. People moved in slow motion, as if under water, the sound of their voices lagging behind the movement of the mouths.

"What'll it be?" a deep male voice asked.

I jumped in my seat. The bartender, a middle-aged guy with an impressive paunch, was asking for my order.

"Didn't mean to scare you," he said.

"Sorry. I...I was kind of spacing out."

"Something to drink?"

"Iced tea." I wanted a shot and a beer, but I needed a clear head given what might lie ahead.

"You're no fun," the rather tipsy woman sitting next to me said. She was younger than I, mid-thirties and attractive. She and her girlfriend appeared to have been doing a nice job putting away glasses of Chardonnay.

"I know. But I'm working."

"Working? It's too late to be working. Have a drink."

"Wish I could."

"What's your name?"

"Ray."

"Hey, Tom, get my good friend Ray here a drink on me, will ya? And none of that ice tea bullshit. Ray, what'll you have?"

Because I was starting to feel self-conscious, and resistance seemed futile, I relented and ordered a Guinness Stout.

"Atta boy," my new friend said. Her shoulder-length hair was dark with light red highlights. She brushed a strand of it back from her face and gave me a smile.

We clinked glasses once my beer arrived, and I thanked her for the drink. Her name was Anne, and her friend, Debra, was chatting up a guy next to her. The two women worked at the insurance company just down the road towards downtown. They came here once a week to blow off steam after work. We talked for a good fifteen minutes. In spite of my circumstances, I found myself attracted to Chardonnay-drinking, insurance-working Anne. The ring finger on her left hand was bare. First Jolene Gillingwater and now Anne. I'd gone decades without having women throw themselves at me, and now in the same week it happened twice. Ray Courage: Chick Magnet. Either that or I was imagining things. I voted for the latter.

"You seem nervous, Ray," Anne said, snapping me back to the moment.

"Sorry. A lot on my mind." I wanted to check my phone again, to see if the GPS trackers had been moved, but Anne moved so close she'd see what I was doing. I didn't really suspect her of being in on the extortion plot. Even so, it felt smarter not to take a chance. She might simply ask about why I had a map pulled up on my phone while I was sitting at a bar. If someone was observing me and overheard her question, the observer might conclude I was tracking the van's location.

After an hour at the bar, Anne's hand now resting well up my thigh, I felt a sense of panic. Not about Anne's hand. I feared I had somehow misread the directions, and now the line of communication with the extortionists had been cut. I pulled my phone out of my pocket, turned away from Anne, and risked a look. The van and the money still sat there, in the parking lot. Something was wrong.

"You're hardly touching your beer," Anne said.

To appease her, I took a sip, set the beer down, and smiled at her. She smiled back and looked deep into my eyes. I took another sip of beer and decided it was time for me to go back to the van, instructions or no instructions from the bad guys. I was about to slide off the barstool when the bartender spoke loud enough to be heard over the sounds inside the room.

"Does anyone here have a van parked at Sand Cove?" he asked after setting down the phone at the back of the bar.

I raised my hand and looked around to see if anyone watched me. No one seemed to care about a guy with a van parked up the road. The bartender approached.

"Not sure why you would have your car parked down at Sand Cove this late this time of year, but I got a call saying you can go move it now. That's all they said."

"Was it a man or a woman?"

He gave me a funny look. "I guess it was a guy. But I could barely hear, and the voice sounded kinda distorted."

This time I made to effort to hide what I was doing when I checked the GPS on my phone. Still no movement. That didn't make any sense to me. Had they abandoned their plan to take the money? Why? Cold feet? Did they fear a setup?

"Why you parked down there?" Anne asked. She removed her hand from my leg, as if anyone who drove a van and parked it in a deserted parking lot might be a bit perverse. A serial killer. A pornographer. Or maybe a coin collector.

"Long story."

The smile she gave me was forced, the kind you might get from a grocery store clerk after she told you "have a nice day." She angled her body away from me and back to the bar. I felt a jab of disappointment. Even in the midst of an illicit twenty million dollar deal, I'd let myself think about a romantic encounter. The human mind goes where it goes. Without another word, I slid off the barstool and left the Virgin Sturgeon.

Fog crept off the river and shrouded the road. I started at a fast walk and then broke into a jog, concerned about what lay ahead at Sand Cove. My mind turned over several possibilities, none of them good for the Monarch team or for me. The deal had gone off the rails for some reason. The more I thought about it, the more I believed one of GPS trackers had been discovered and scared them off. I hadn't told Wiggin or anyone else about putting the trackers on the van and inside the money. They'd be upset with me for doing so. My motives had been worthy. Worthy or not, it appeared I'd cost the Monarch team the chance to retrieve their project.

When I arrived at the parking lot fifteen minutes later, the van sat in the same spot where I'd left it. The driver's door was locked. I found the keys underneath the van and unlocked it. I opened the rear door of the van. All of the mailbags were gone. They'd been replaced by a large cardboard box adorned with the Heavenly Soft Toilet Tissue logo. Twenty million dollars just bought us a case of toilet paper.

It was difficult to see inside the box in the darkness, so I used the flashlight app on my phone. I folded back the top flaps, shone the light inside, and saw six objects—my five GPS tracking devices and a thin metal box about one foot by two feet.

Forty minutes later, Ken Wiggin, Candace Symington, and I assembled in Wiggin's office. A few minutes after that, the director of technology arrived. It was eleven o'clock and he was grumpy, though his mood brightened when he saw the object on Wiggin's desk.

"Is that what I think it is?" he asked.

"That's why we called you," Wiggin said.

We followed him to the administration building, where he unlocked the front door and led us to the university's server room. Fifteen minutes later, we were all giving each other high fives.

It had cost twenty million dollars. But the Monarch Project had been recovered.

twenty

BY THE TIME I ARRIVED home it was after one in the morning. I poured myself three fingers of bourbon, cracked open a beer, and slumped into a chair in my living room. Sometime later I drifted to sleep.

The nightmares returned. The men convulsed each time a round from my gun penetrated their flesh, the epic violence playing out in slow motion, the events of several seconds stretching out into minutes, over and over again. Then Thomas Chan's bloodied, disfigured body came into view in Technicolor vividness. Chan lay there on his blood-stained bed. He spoke to me, his eyes dead, his mouth moving up and down like a puppet's. "You did this," he said, raising his bloodied hand and flipping me off with that middle finger. "You, you, you…"

The banging on the door cast away the image and awakened me. I had fallen asleep in the living room. The beer and whiskey glasses were both empty. Morning light came in from the front window. I picked up my cell phone from the coffee table to check the time. It was a little past seven in the morning. The screen indicated I had five missed calls and voice mails from Granderson University.

Jerry Langford greeted me when I opened the door.

"What the fuck!" he said as soon as he saw me, his face wild-eyed, spittle flying from his mouth.

"Good morning to you, too, Jerry. Would you like to come in?"

"No!"

"Is it me or is something troubling you?"

"How could you do that? You paid twenty million dollars to an extortionist?"

I held up my phone and showed it to him. "Are these calls from you?"

"Bet your ass they are. You've been dodging my calls. Why do you think I'm here?"

"Look, I'm sorry I couldn't keep you in the loop. It's what the project people wanted. They said if—"

"I don't care what Wiggin wanted. You were working for *me*. You were to find out what was going on and report back to *me*."

"I was going to do it today." I really was, but in the moment it sounded ridiculous.

He bore a hole in me with his seething eyes. "I'm going to have to report this to the administration. They're going to be incensed. I'll be lucky if I keep my job."

"Are you sure that's a good idea?"

"Of course it is. I have no choice."

"I'm not so sure Sunrise and NAFC are going to want it known they paid off an extortionist. That's a bad precedent for them to set. And it makes the university look bad."

"If the university wants to keep a lid on it then that's up to the president or the board of trustees. But I need to tell them."

He was right. I hoped the administration had the good sense to not release the information to the media. Nothing good would come of that. The elation I'd felt the night before about retrieving Monarch morphed into something else in the light of morning. Yes, we'd retrieved the project. But we'd given into criminal demands. How could doing so possibly reflect well on any of us involved? Selfishly, I thought about what that might do to my reputation. Not only had I signed off on paying the ransom money, I'd been the one who'd delivered it. Aside from what our actions might do to our reputations, how could we be assured the SCS or whoever was behind the plot would not come back to steal the project a second time?

"How did you find out about the payment?"

"I got a phone call."

"From whom?"

"Never mind."

"And you came all the way out here from Granderson to thank me for my great work."

"I came out here to fire your sorry ass. You are never to set foot on the Granderson campus again. Do you understand?"

"It's an easy concept to grasp."

"And if I can find a way to bust your ass or to sue you, you'd better be ready because that's my top priority right now."

"Can I get you a cup of coffee, Jerry? You seem a bit stressed."

He stormed off and appeared not to hear my "drive safely" as he did so.

My firing put an exclamation point on the entire Monarch case. With Monarch's return and Granderson cutting me loose, the Thomas Chan investigation was up to the police to handle, not me. Yet, something didn't feel right about that. Maybe it was the unease I felt about paying the ransom and then getting tongue-lashed by Langford. Yeah, that was part of it. But there was more. I shut the door and leaned back against it trying to get my mind around why I didn't have a good feeling about any of it. Nothing came clear. Except that I needed a good breakfast and at least two cups of strong coffee.

After clearing my breakfast dishes, I showered, dressed, and headed out to run a few errands before my eleven o'clock appointment with Dr. Beckly, the shrink Dr. Nelson had referred me to. It was about nine-thirty, as I was parking in the grocery store lot, when my phone rang.

"Ray?" came the woman's voice after I picked up.

"Yes."

"It's Jolene. Jolene Gillingwater. From Sacramento Oaks."

A pause. "Hi." I tried to inject enthusiasm into my voice. I'd forgotten she had my phone number from the information sheet I'd filled out at her country club.

"I don't mean to sound forward, or at least more forward than you must already think I am, but I was going to be in your part of town around lunchtime and was wondering if we could get together."

Crap. Think. Think. "Um, I have a doctor's appointment at eleven."

"That's okay. I won't be done with my errands until around twelve or twelve-thirty. Can you meet me at Hana Tsubaki about twelve forty-five?"

"Sure."

We ended the call, and I cursed myself for not anticipating it and having prepared a better excuse. Now I was committed to a lunch date with Danny Cashmore's girlfriend.

Rubia called as I sat in the car in front of Dr. Frank Beckly's office. My appointment with the psychiatrist wasn't for another ten minutes, so I used the time to fill her in on everything that happened the night before, culminating in the successful return of Monarch.

"You don't sound happy about it," she said.

"For one thing, I got fired by Granderson's security chief."

"So what? The deal was over."

"In a sense, yeah."

"What the hell, 'in a sense'? Over is over."

"There's Chan," I said.

"Yeah, and the cops are working that. And I thought you said he was a prick."

"Doesn't mean someone can get away with killing him."

"Righteous Ray."

"So why'd you call?"

"You're not big on small talk today," she said.

"I'm a bit cranky. I'll give you that."

"You're always a bit cranky. Today I'd say you're freakin' ornery."

I shook my head. If I believed I had a finite number of words to utter in my lifetime, I was wasting a precious bundle in this conversation.

"Getting back to my question," I said. "Why did you call?"

"Thought you'd never ask. First thing, I found out about Benzer's parents. They live up in Oroville. The dad runs a little liquor store. The mom's disabled. From what I can tell they don't have much. The two of them live above the liquor store in a little one-bedroom apartment. They drive a twenty-year-old Corolla."

"How'd you find this out?"

"Got connections in Chico who got connections in Oroville."

"Have."

"What?"

"You *have* connections in Chico who *have* connections in Oroville."

"That's what I said."

There was no hope. "Go on."

"That's it. They're poor or pretty darn close to it."

"Maybe they've got millions squirreled away in a mattress," I said.

"Not likely. The liquor store is mortgaged to the hilt. They don't have squat."

I started to end the call, when Rubia interrupted me.

"Hey, I've got more. Got the scoop on the *chica*, Jolene Gilling-whatever."

"Gillingwater. Jolene Gillingwater."

"Whatever. Anyway, she checks out." Rubia ran through Jolene's employment dates at Los Altos Country Club, Pebble Beach, Auburn Hills and Sacramento Oaks. She graduated magna cum laude from Cal State, Monterey Bay and lettered in golf for four years. Her credit ratings were top notch and she owned her home in Sacramento's Greenhaven neighborhood. She'd been married once, her husband died of cancer ten years ago. No kids.

I cursed when she'd finished.

"What's the matter?" she asked. "She's about perfect."

Perfect. Except she'd hit on me. And now we were going on a date. The question I grappled with now was how to tell Danny Cashmore.

I got out of the car and walked into the medical building on Scripps Drive. Dr. Beckly's office was on the third floor. As I waited at the elevator, I thought more about my dreams the night before. The dreams felt different this time, especially the shooting sequence. I wasn't sure what it meant, but I knew it meant something. A bell dinged announcing the arrival of the elevator car. I turned and walked out of the building, giving me a little over an hour and a half to figure out how to handle my date with Jolene.

twenty-one

HANA TSUBAKI RESTAURANT'S PARKING LOT, a long narrow strip of asphalt off J Street in east Sacramento, was packed. I squeezed into a spot between a Ferrari and a Tesla and worried whether their owners might insist I relocate until a more suitable car could ease between the two alpha vehicles. When I noted an Accord on the other side of the Tesla and a Jetta next to the Ferrari, I felt relieved vehicular mediocrity still reigned in this part of town.

My fingers hovered over the keypad on my cell phone. I wanted to call Rubia to see if she had anything more about the Golden Dragons. Thomas Chan's murder still nagged me. I had tried doing some Internet research, but turned up just a small mention in Wikipedia under Asian Gangs. Though I did want to learn more about the Dragons and their methods of operation, the real reason I wanted to call Rubia was for moral support, maybe even an offer to join Jolene and me for lunch.

By my watch, I was five minutes early for our appointed date. I spent the time trying to decide whether to confess to working for Danny Cashmore at the start of lunch or at the end. Either way, it would be awkward. Danny wouldn't like it, and I wouldn't blame him. But it was more important to be straight up with Jolene and with Danny, as uncomfortable as doing so would be for me.

I walked through the doors at precisely twelve forty-five. Though not large, the restaurant packed in a good-sized crowd whose amiable chatter filled the space. Several light box sculptures served as both art and light source in the center of the room, while the dark wood paneling and shoji screens completed an Asian ambience. Jolene sat at one of the simple wooden tables set for two.

"I hope I didn't keep you waiting long," I said upon reaching the table.

"You're right on time." She had a glass of white wine in front of her. I liked her confidence, ordering alcohol without worrying what I would think. She wore a simple black silk blouse with a loose collar parted slightly above her sternum. The sparkle from her diamond stud earrings contrasted with the blouse. In the six days since we'd seen each other, I'd obsessed so much about breaking things to Danny I'd forgotten how attractive Jolene was.

"You're a woman after my own heart." I pointed at her wine, immediately regretting the comment. I needed to create distance not connection with this woman.

"How've you been?" she asked once I settled in my seat.

"Good." So much had happened since our last meeting. The story about delivering the money to the extortionist could fill up two lunch dates. Then there was the earlier Thomas Chan murder I could regale her with. But I wasn't here to impress. Polite small talk would be the strategy. "How about you?"

She reached across the table and put her hand over mine. It felt good, even better than the roving hand Anne had placed on my thigh the night before. "I hope you don't think it was forward of me to call you. I normally wouldn't do that. Giving you my number the other day wasn't usual for me either. You probably don't believe me, but it's true." She looked at me with those clear blue eyes, and I felt myself getting drawn in.

I smiled. "I don't think it's forward at all. I'm flattered you think enough of me to want to have lunch. Thank you."

The waitress arrived, a petite Japanese woman with a heavy but cute accent. I ordered a Sapporo beer and asked for another minute on the menu before deciding on lunch.

"Now that the awkwardness is over, do you mind if I ask a little bit more about you?"

I did mind, but what could I say? "Of course."

"You're a private investigator. You didn't mention it the other day."

I could feel my face heat up, and I hoped I didn't redden. "You're good with a web browser."

"I saw the article in the Sac State student newspaper about your retirement. Three-time winner of the school's teacher-of-the-year award during your career. Not bad."

"I had my moments." I wanted my beer to arrive.

"If you were such a good teacher, why did you retire? You're not that old."

I smiled at her, a goofy "I don't know how to say this" smile. "I was accused of sexual harassment."

"Oh." She sat back in her chair and put her hands in her lap.

"I suppose I should explain."

"If you're comfortable doing so." Realizing her instinctive reaction to my earlier statement, she moved forward again, resting one forearm on the table as she took hold of the stem of her wine glass.

"I don't want to bore you with all the specifics, so I'll give you the summary version. A student of mine was getting an F in one of my classes. She asked if performing a certain sexual act on me would earn her an A. The proposition shocked me. I told her no and then failed her in the course because she hadn't done the work. She then went to the communications department chair and told him I had groped her after class one night and asked her to have sex."

"So it was a he said, she said thing."

"Very much so. The university launched a full investigation. Under careful scrutiny, she couldn't get her story straight and kept contradicting herself. What's more, the student had a history of less than stellar behavior. She'd been suspended from two previous colleges for plagiarism and cheating. In the end, they found me innocent of the accusation."

"Must have been stressful for you."

"It was. I hope you don't think I'm some sort of deviant or something."

She laughed. "What was the sex act she offered?" She took a sip of wine.

"Do you really want to know?"

"No, that's okay, I'll save you the embarrassment."

"Thank you."

"Oral sex, right?"

"You're something else." I nodded my head and laughed.

"At least you can laugh about it now."

My beer arrived, and I took a long sip. How had I allowed the conversation to go to my sexual harassment case?

"Is that why you retired? The accusations?"

"Pretty much. Even though I was exonerated, students talked. My colleagues were even worse. Whispering behind my back. That kind of thing. I didn't want to deal with it anymore, so I took my pension and left."

"Which brings us back to you now being a private investigator. Why didn't you say something about it?"

"I don't know." Though I did. I didn't want her to put in her mind I might be investigating her as marriage material for Danny. "I've only been at it a year and have just a handful of clients. I'd call myself more of a dabbler at this point than a professional."

She smiled. "You're modest. I saw you were in a shootout. That sounded amazing. And I read about the case you worked on for Lionel Stroud. It's all pretty impressive stuff."

"Again with the Internet, huh?" I drank half my beer.

"I know. It sounds like I'm stalking you or something. Just curious is all. A girl can't be too careful when she asks someone to lunch."

I refrained from telling her I knew all her employment start and stop dates, when she earned her college degree, her credit scores, how much she owed on her house in Greenhaven, and that she was widowed ten years earlier.

"Have you been married?" she asked. "Or is that too personal of a question to ask on a first lunch date?"

"Once. My wife died a little over thirteen years ago. Our daughter Sara is in her second year at UCLA Law School. I miss them both."

"I lost my husband ten years ago. To cancer. I know what you mean. I still miss him, too."

"I'm sorry." I cast my eyes to the table in front of me, an image of my wife Pam forming in my mind. As usual, she was smiling, the full of life smile that had drawn me to her in the first place, long ago during our undergraduate days at San Jose State. When I raised my eyes from the table, Jolene's eyes seemed a bit distant, as if she too had evoked a memory of her spouse.

The waitress arrived and we ordered. Jolene ordered teriyaki chicken, and I ordered the sesame beef and California roll bento box. When I ordered another beer, Jolene hemmed and hawed about a second glass of wine before deciding to join me.

"Are you seeing anyone now?" she asked.

"You do get to the point. I will say that."

"I figure at my age, I'm through being coy, playing games, or beating around the bush."

I nodded. "No. My last relationship ended a year ago." I saw no need to elaborate, deciding months ago to never bare the details of my last romance. "How about you?"

She looked down at her lap and then started to reach for her wine, but the waitress had already removed her empty glass. "I am seeing someone."

"Really?"

"Yes." She looked up at me, and we locked eyes. "He's a nice guy, but he sees more in the relationship than I do. We've gone out a couple of months now. I have a good time with him. He's funny, smart, and likes to do fun things. But I can't see myself with him long term. I'm planning on breaking it off with him later this week as a matter of fact. He's hinted at us maybe getting married, so it's not fair to keep things going the way they are."

"You don't see a future with this guy?" This was my chance to bring up my connection to Danny, to come clean about how I really ended up meeting her at Sacramento Oaks. I started to speak, but Jolene spoke first.

"No." She shook her head. "I don't see a future with him."

Again, it was time for me to tell her the truth. "I should proba-bly—"

The arrival of our waitress with our food and drinks interrupted me. She placed Jolene's order in front of me, and mine in front of Jolene. By the time we sorted it all out, I'd lost my inclination to bring up Danny, and Jolene appeared to have forgotten I'd started to say something moments before.

A silence set in as we ate. A minute or two passed, the silence on the verge of awkward. We both reached for our drinks and took long sips. When we saw each other doing so, we laughed.

"Sorry, Ray. When I invited you to lunch I was thinking some light conversation, maybe talk a little golf, a little weather, and a bit of 'what about those Kings?' sprinkled in, but there's something about you."

"What about those Kings?" I said. We laughed again.

For the next half hour, we enjoyed our food and stayed away from serious topics. Once I decided not to talk about Danny and to simply enjoy being with this attractive and engaging woman, the lunch became a pleasure, albeit a guilty one. I knew this wasn't a good idea. I knew nothing good would come from Jolene falling for me. I just couldn't help myself; I was having a good time and didn't want to ruin it. After our plates were cleared, we finished our drinks and ordered coffee. By now, most of the restaurant had emptied.

"You're kind of intriguing, Ray. I can't figure out if you're shy, or modest, or what. But I get the sense there's more to you than meets the eye."

"You're overthinking this. I'm pretty much a simpleton." I wasn't referring to my inability to be forthcoming about Danny, but I probably should have been.

"Oh, I doubt that."

She offered to pay the bill because she had invited me to lunch. Call me sexist or old school, but I insisted on paying. Besides, I had a wonderful time. Too wonderful. Jolene was, after all, dating my friend. At least for the moment. For that reason alone, I told myself, I had to keep a respectful distance.

We walked out to the parking lot, the Ferrari and Tesla long gone. The Jetta I'd spotted earlier was hers.

"I had a good time," she said. "Let's do this again." She hesitated a beat before she leaned in and kissed me on the lips. And I kissed her back, a kiss that lasted too long and brought too much enjoyment.

So much for my keeping a respectful distance.

twenty-two

NO ONE ANSWERED THE PHONE at Chan International. I punched in the number for Benzer's cell phone Langford had given me earlier. Langford. Though a gasbag, he deserved an apology. Looking back on the past week, things had moved so fast and the Monarch team had been steadfast about keeping a lid on the extortion. Still, Langford had hired me and asked to be kept in the loop. I'd call him once he cooled off in a day or two to explain and apologize.

Benzer's phone rang seven times before going to voicemail. I wondered if he recognized my number and was avoiding my call. I had called him before on his cell, so even if caller ID didn't pop my name, he might recognize the number.

With the Granderson job completed, and with no other paying gigs, I had time on my hands. I should have let go of Chan, SCS, and everything else related to Granderson. I just couldn't. A dead young man. A twenty-million-dollar ransom. An angry client in Langford. More questions than answers. Nothing about where things stood satisfied me.

First, I tried Benzer's apartment without success. During the ten-minute drive to Chan International, my mind kept returning to my lunch with Jolene. I tried to rationalize my returning her kiss, knowing full well I was kidding myself. She had kissed me first, I told myself. No, I could have stopped it, making it a peck on the mouth instead of a romantic lip lock. She was planning on breaking up with Danny. So what? She was still dating my friend, and I owed it to him to keep my lips off his girlfriend. I liked her. That was irrelevant. Even though I liked her, Danny had hired me to investigate her, not kiss her. I shook my head and sighed a dozen times as I drove and, somehow, I sensed the whole Danny-Jolene business would not turn out well for any of us.

Four cars were parked on the street near the entrance to Chan International, though I didn't know if any of them belonged to Benzer. The front door to the office wasn't locked. I entered a small lobby with an empty reception desk, behind which stood an entryway to the offices. I walked around the desk and through the entry into an open office space with two desks on opposite walls. Benzer was kneeling down on the far side of one desk. I knocked on the top of a nearby bookshelf to avoid startling him.

"What the hell are you doing here?" He stood and took two steps towards me as if not wanting me to see what he'd been doing. He was wearing a dark gray business suit, with a sharp-looking maroon tie.

"Why did you lie to me?" I asked.

"What the are you talking about?"

"About the money for the payoffs." I moved farther into the room, next to the desk on the opposite wall from Benzer's. "You said your parents loaned you the money. Your parents don't have that kind of money to lend you."

"How would you know?" He moved his body as I walked across the room, tracking me. "And I don't like you snooping into my business. You're not a cop. You don't have any right to harass me."

"This isn't harassment. If I wanted to harass you, it wouldn't be as pleasant as this."

"Oh, you're a real badass."

"No, I'm not saying that. I just don't like it when people lie to me, especially when I might be working to help find whoever killed your business partner. The only reason someone might lie is if they have something to hide. So what are you hiding, Adam?"

He glanced over to where he'd been kneeling. When he did so, I moved two steps over and could see a small safe, its door open an inch, and a black nylon briefcase next to it.

"I've got nothing to hide. I just don't like sharing information with strangers who have no reason to have that information."

"Doing a little banking?" I gestured at the safe.

"That's what I'm talking about. You keep sticking your nose where it doesn't belong."

"You know, I'm getting tired of this. You're acting like a sullen teenager. So, I'm going to try to move the conversation along." I stepped to within arm's reach of him and looked him in the eyes. "Here's what I think. You and Thomas Chan, freshly minted MBAs, were playing business. Create a website with embellished bios and client lists, rent an office, lease some furniture, get some fancy suits, and even buy yourself a cool little safe. Then somewhere along the way, you guys found out running a business needs two things—money and clients. Somehow, you found some money to try and buy clients. Then things got a little dicey. Maybe you borrowed the money and couldn't pay it back. Maybe one of your clients got mad at you for some reason. I'm not sure exactly what happened, but you and Chan somehow ticked somebody off. They killed Chan over it. And now I'm guessing they want something from you."

"You have no clue what you're talking about." He faked a laugh and tried to affect an indignant expression. A phone trilled, and he reached into a side pocket of the suit to retrieve his cell. He looked at the number on the screen, shook his head, silenced the ringer, and returned the phone to his pocket.

"Important call? You can take it if you want. It won't offend me."

"Look, if it will help get you out of my hair, I'll admit it. I lied about where we got the money to pay off the Chinese. My parents didn't lend it to me. I told you that so you'd go away. The money was ours, Chan International's. It was our profits from our other clients. You have to invest money to make money, and that's how we saw the payoffs. As investments. Simple as that."

"You and Chan made over a hundred and fifty thousand dollars in profit in just a few months after graduation?"

"We started the business even before we graduated, so we had cash flow."

"I'm not buying it. I think you're in some trouble. It could be the same trouble that got Chan killed. Or it could be you had something to do with him getting killed."

He looked away and drew back a step. He seemed to be running something through his mind. When he looked at me, he shook his head. "I didn't have anything to do with Thomas's murder. That's ludicrous. Everybody knows he and I were good friends. And neither of us was in any kind of trouble."

"Then why were the Golden Dragons staking out Thomas's house the day before he was killed?"

"What's a Golden Dragon?" It was a nice try, but I could tell I'd hit a nerve; his previous bluster deflated.

"Are they into you for some money? Are they brokering a deal?"

"I don't know what you're talking about. You're going to have to go now. I have to close up the office and head to an appointment." He turned his back on me and made a show of riffling through some papers on his desk.

"Be careful, Adam," I said and walked out of the office.

Three crows squawked from the telephone wire above my car, as if Benzer had hired them to shoo me off. Maybe he wasn't up to something. Maybe he didn't have anything to do with Chan's death. Maybe Rubia had been wrong and the guy in the Camaro near Chan's house wasn't a Chinese mobster, just some guy waiting for a friend. Benzer wasn't going to help me determine what was or wasn't. At least not voluntarily.

When he emerged from his office ten minutes later, I slunk down in my car seat and peered over the top of the steering wheel as Benzer locked the office door. He carried the nylon brief case in one hand, tossing it into the back seat of a white Lexus before getting in the car and driving off. I let him drive about a block before I pulled out from the curb to follow.

He turned right onto Stockton Boulevard heading south before making a left a few blocks later onto T Street, a leafy thoroughfare lined with Tudor and craftsman homes, a wide greenbelt separating the eastbound and westbound traffic lanes. We continued east for a mile until we reached 59th Street, where Benzer turned left and I followed. By now, I knew where he was going.

A few minutes later, he pulled into the visitor parking circle in front of SMUD's headquarters building on S Street. I pulled over on S and watched as he parked his car in the circle. A few seconds later, he was walking towards the building entrance, briefcase in hand. He paused for a second in front of the glass next to the door to straighten his tie and check himself out from head to toe.

When he disappeared into the building, I debated whether to stay or to leave, deciding an hour or so more invested in Benzer might be worth it. My guess was he had come to visit with Roger Talbert, maybe to reassure him his business with the Chinese printing company was fine in the wake of Chan's death.

Because I was stopped in a red zone on the street, I drove into the parking circle and found a space close enough to observe Benzer's car but far enough away so he couldn't spot me. I whiled away the time looking through my windshield, admiring the Wayne Thiebaud mosaic tile artwork adorning the building's first floor wall. I read an article about it years before. The work was the famed artist's only public piece of art, and he'd done it for a modest fee in the 1950s, when his career was just starting. As much as I wanted to appreciate the work up close, I couldn't risk Benzer seeing me, so I remained slouched in my car listening to KNBR as a sports talk host and his callers sang the praises of the San Francisco Giants and their chances for winning another World Series title.

About an hour later—just after four o'clock—Benzer emerged from the building and got into his car. He drove west on S Street, crossed 59th and merged onto Highway 50, the westbound lands starting to clog with commuters. I kept one car between his Lexus and my car as we passed the Highway 99 exit and took the 26th Street off ramp. As we neared 21st Street, he slowed, making a left turn at V Street. A few seconds later, I made the same turn on V and saw his car parked in front of a small house wedged between two much larger ones.

He was knocking on the door of the house as I drove by. I parked up the street and walked back to the house. The home was older, small, white with blue trim, a picture window in the front, drapes drawn behind it. A narrow driveway ran along the side of the house. On it were parked a newer black Chevy Camaro and an older Ford, tricked out in low-rider mode.

I walked past the house and stopped to look up and down the street. Not a soul was out and about. I went up the driveway to the first window nearest the street. The curtains were drawn, but there was enough of a gap to offer a view inside.

Benzer and two Asian men sat at a kitchen table. Benzer was talking and the two other men were sitting back in their chairs, arms crossed, faces stern. Benzer seemed to be growing more animated the more he spoke. I could hear his voice through the window but couldn't make out the actual words. A few moments later, he reached inside his briefcase and pulled out two stacks of bills, which he plopped onto the table.

The two men exchanged glances and shook their heads.

twenty-three

THE TWO OF THEM CONTINUED shaking their heads. The older one sitting across from Benzer seemed to be in charge. He was about thirty, on the chunky side, with a round, shaved head and a mustache and goatee. He wore a black T-shirt with a thick silver chain around his neck that dangled down to the middle of his chest. I couldn't tell if this was the same guy who'd been sitting in the car near Chan's house, though the diamond earring in his left ear suggested it was. The other guy was maybe twenty and appeared to be looking for some direction as he sat smoking a cigarette, his eyes locked on the older man. This guy wore a black New York Yankees baseball cap and a white wife beater, revealing tattoos running down one arm from shoulder to wrist. Both of them had handguns tucked into the waist of their jeans.

The kitchen was cluttered with dirty plates, pots, and pans. Beyond it were the living and dining areas that comprised the entire front of the house. As far as I could tell, it was just Benzer and the two men in the house. I thought about going around to the back to confirm this but didn't think it prudent to risk being seen or to abandon my view of Benzer.

Black T-shirt gave Wife Beater a slight nod. The younger man stubbed out his cigarette in an ashtray, stood, and locked Benzer in a chokehold, lifting him up out of the chair. T-shirt screamed at Benzer, pointing a finger within inches of the victim's terrified face. Benzer strained to free himself, but Wife Beater was strong for such a skinny kid.

Benzer pleaded, his voice whiney and loud. The older gangbanger pummeled Benzer; three punches to the face drew blood from a cut under the eye and from the nose. Black T-shirt followed those blows with two vicious uppercuts to the gut. Benzer started to crumble, but Wife Beater held Benzer up and set him back into the chair.

Black T-shirt went to a kitchen drawer and pulled out a box of plastic wrap. He opened a second drawer and extracted a large meat cleaver. With meticulous care, he rolled out a couple of feet of plastic wrap and placed it along the edge of the table. When he said something to Benzer, he shook his head. Tears streamed down his cheeks, mixing with the blood covering the entire right side of his face. Maintaining the chokehold, Wife Beater reached over with his free hand and grabbed Benzer's right wrist and put it on the table, whispering something into his ear. A few seconds later, Benzer placed his unsteady index finger on the edge of the table over the sheet of plastic as his body quaked. T-shirt raised the meat cleaver above his shoulder.

I turned and sprinted for the front door, bounding up the two porch steps, pausing for a count of two to take a breath and to pull out my gun from its holster. I tested the doorknob and found it unlocked. I had to decide whether to burst in, using surprise as my ally, or sneak in. From what I could tell from my previous view at the window, they didn't have a line of sight to the front door. I eased the door open and stuck my head inside. Benzer was wailing while one of the men shouted.

"You disrespect me! You disrespect Bo! You disrespect Golden Dragons!"

"Nooooo," Benzer said, more of a howl than a word.

I had to assume they were preparing to cut off at least one finger, as they had with Chan. As I entered the kitchen's doorway, the older man still had the cleaver above his shoulder, ready to hack at Benzer's index finger which the other man had pinned to the table.

"Stop!" I said leveling the gun at the man with the cleaver. "Put it down!"

He thought for a moment before lowering the cleaver and dropping it to the floor. I turned the gun on Wife Beater. "You, let him go. And don't try anything."

He released the chokehold and his grip on Benzer's hand.

"Both of you, ease those guns out of your jeans and drop them."

They hesitated. I took dead aim at Black T-shirt. "I'll do it."

He reached in for the gun and bent down to place it on the floor. A few seconds later, the second man did the same.

"Who the fuck are you?" Black T-shirt said.

"Ray will do for now."

"Well, Ray, you're going to regret this, man. You back out of here now, I might forget it. Do you know who I am?" When I didn't reply, he continued. "I'm Wu Wing, and you don't want to fuck with me. Tell him, Bo," he said to the younger man.

"You don't want to fuck with him," Bo said.

"That's articulate of you, Bo. The way you took his words and made them your own. You'll go far in the Golden Dragon Dynasty."

"So you're a funny man on top of being stupid," Wu said.

"I have my moments. Now kick those guns towards me."

Bo scowled, and Wu shook his head. But when I swept my gun across the room from Wu to Bo and then back, the older man nodded. With their feet, they slid the guns across the floor towards me. I picked up one gun, then the other, stuffing them into my coat pockets.

"You," I said to Wu. "Fill a plastic bag with ice."

He moved slowly to the same drawer from which he'd removed the plastic wrap. I took a couple of steps back so I could keep both men within easy shooting sight. "Benzer, get over here."

Benzer shot up from the kitchen table and scrambled beside me; his nose was crooked, almost at a right angle from normal. He bent at the waist in obvious pain. As instructed, Wu went to the refrigerator and opened the top door to the freezer. I heard him rattle around some ice and then watched him stick a handful of it into the plastic bag.

"Toss it over here. Easy."

The bag landed at my feet. I picked it up, keeping my eyes and the gun on both of them. I handed the bag to Benzer. "Use this on your nose."

I wanted to tie them up, to give us a chance to escape. The condition he was in, Benzer would be no help with that. I spotted a couple of kitchen towels on the counter next to the sink. I grabbed them, handing one to Benzer and told him to use it to clean up his face. I tossed the second towel towards Bo.

"Bo, my man, pick up that towel and tear it into three or four long strips."

He didn't want to do it. He gave me the baddest, hard-assed look he could muster before grabbing the towel.

"By the way, those tatts look nice on you. Combined with the wife beater it gives you a certain *je ne sais quois,* urban gangbanger but with a tinge of elfishness. It's cute."

He did not find my banter amusing. If I had any sense, I wouldn't have provoked him, but I was sick of people like him; a little derision seemed the least he deserved. He glared at me, using his rising anger to rip the towel into four pieces.

"Good. Now tie your man Wu's hands behind his back, and then do the same with his feet. And don't tie some wimpy little knots. I'm watching you. Wu, take a seat."

Bo did as instructed. Wu, seated in a kitchen chair, watched his underling tie him up. "You're going to be a dead man when this is over," he said.

"Have you tried yoga?" I asked. "It's supposed to be a great stress reliever. And it might even help with the gut you're starting to grow there. I'd think about trying it if I were you. It might reduce some of the hostility you feel from time to time."

As expected, he dropped an F-bomb on me.

"Let's get out of here," Benzer said, his jaw flexed tight in pain.

"Hold on. Bo, I don't like the knot on his feet. Use another strip and tie one of his legs to a chair."

"I don't feel so good," Benzer said, his voice weak and trembling.

Once I was satisfied with the quality of Bo's knots, I told him to take his clothes off. I didn't have two free hands to tie him up, and Benzer couldn't do it. I figured having him strip naked might keep him from running down the street after us.

Reluctantly, Bo stripped down to his underwear.

"Take those off."

He hesitated.

"Don't worry, I won't look at your pee pee."

Once he slid off his underwear, he covered his privates with his two hands.

I turned to Benzer and whispered into his ear. "Get the hell out of here. Head east on V Street and you'll see my car—it's blue—about a half a block on the right. Get in the passenger seat, and I'll be there in a minute."

He headed to the front door, stumbling a couple of times. I feared he might faint, but he appeared to regain some strength when he reached the door. I gave him about a minute to make it to my car and then started to back out of the kitchen.

"The second he leaves, you shoot his ass, Bo," Wu said. As I had suspected, the two guns in my pocket were not all the firearms in the house. I didn't want to take the time to find their stash of guns and knew they wouldn't be any help in locating them.

"Bet your ass," he replied.

When I reached the front door, I eased my way outside, my gun trained on Bo until I closed the door and ran towards my car. Halfway to my car, I looked over my shoulder to see naked Bo racking a shotgun fifty feet away. A second later, I heard the blast. I continued to run, making it to the car as another blast from the shotgun rang out. I fishtailed out from the curb, down V Street and away from Bo, who fired a third volley even though we were far out of range.

The nearest emergency room was six blocks away, but I couldn't risk going there. The two Golden Dragons would probably check the closest hospital first.

"You all right?" I asked.

"Peachy." Benzer was bent over in the passenger seat. "Goddamn this hurts."

We headed towards a hospital across town over in Carmichael. If they decided to look for us at emergency rooms, this would be fourth or fifth on the list, which I hoped would be enough time to get Benzer treated. I couldn't count on that alone.

I called Sac PD's main number and asked for Nick Trujillo. He picked up his line a few seconds later, his usual charming self.

"What the fuck do you want, Courage?"

"It's a pleasure to talk to you, too."

"What do you want?"

"Just saw a naked guy shooting a shotgun on the 2100 block of V Street. Third house in from the corner. If you look into it closely, you might find they are members of an Asian gang called the Golden Dragons wanting to establish a foothold here. This could be your chance to nip that in the bud. They beat the hell out of a guy named Adam Benzer. I'm taking him to the emergency room at Sutter Carmichael. You may want to send a uniform to see him there."

He tried to push me for details on why I knew so much about the gangsters, but I told him I had to hang up. Trujillo would get back to me later, and I hoped if my call turned into a significant arrest for him it would offset how pissed off he was at the moment for cutting him off.

"What was that business all about?" I asked. "Why were you giving them money?"

The pain must have weakened his will to stonewall me because he replied without hesitating. "Interest."

"Let me guess, you borrowed money from them to bribe your clients and the Chinese companies."

He nodded. "Fucking Thomas's idea. Borrowed five hundred thousand. Said we'd make it back in a couple of days and pay it all back."

"How the hell were you going to do that?"

"Said he had a deal lined up." His voice was thick with pain. "But it fell through. And we owed fifty thousand a week in interest. Can you drive any faster?"

"What happened to the original amount?"

"We spent most of it on bribes. I had twenty-five grand left in the safe. That's what I gave them. Thought it would be okay. They were pissed I shorted them."

"What's the deal Chan had that fell through?"

"Don't know."

He was lying. A two-person business takes on a risky loan betting on a major deal to make them rich, and one of the partners doesn't know what the deal is? "Why did you go to SMUD today?"

He looked over at me from his doubled-over position. "Following up on the printing contract. Wanted to let them know it's still cool. Even without Thomas."

I drove to the ambulance port in front of the emergency room entrance. I went around to the side of the car and helped Benzer out. We headed towards the glass doors when I stopped and returned to the car, opened the trunk, and tossed the three guns inside.

Thirty minutes later, Benzer was admitted to the emergency room. I hoped the doctors could fix his nose and wondered if he had significant internal injuries. When I walked out of the emergency room entrance, I felt relatively secure, certain Bo and Wu had not tracked me down. At least not yet.

twenty-four

THE NEXT MORNING I AWOKE to rain pounding my roof so hard I gave up falling back to sleep at five o'clock. I retrieved the *Sacramento Bee* from the front porch, started a half pot of coffee, and then watched through my kitchen window as the rain slanted across the sky, peppering the landscape faster than the drains could handle. From previous rainstorms, I knew another hour like this would flood the street. Gusts of wind battered the trees and power lines, issuing a low-pitched howl, adding voice to the visual and physical assault of the earth.

Watching the storm, I wondered about Adam Benzer. Had he spent the night in the hospital? How severe were his injuries? Was he holding anything else from me? He and Thomas Chan had gotten in over their heads, costing Chan his life—and Benzer, a beating.

I put two pieces of wheat toast in the toaster and dropped two eggs into the small pan I'd filled with water. I turned on the gas burner to get the water boiling. The expiration date on the orange juice was a day overdue, so I filled my juice glass and dumped the rest of it in the sink. I took a sip and eyed the prescription bottle on the shelf above the counter. It'd been over a week since my appointment with Dr. Nelson. I regretted going to see him. There had been the nightmares and the day visions. Those had been real. In the days since my appointment, my subconscious had turned over the troubling violent events and transformed them into something else. I smiled and shook my head.

I read the paper while I ate the soft boiled eggs on toast and drank the coffee. The Sacramento Kings, as usual, were on track not to make the NBA playoffs. The Giants avoided arbitration and agreed to terms with their left fielder on a one-year, eight-million-dollar deal. The guy hit under .250 with three home runs and he gets eight million? Sure wish I could have hit a curve ball in high school. I might have gone on to make more in one season than in twenty-three years of teaching. I searched twice through the front page and the Our Region section of the paper but found no mention of an arrest of two Asian gang members. Damn.

After breakfast, I went online, logged into my Intellius account, and typed in the name Riley Forrester, the pitchfork-wielding sociology professor. I jotted down his address and then entered it at the progessive.com website. The website revealed Forrester drove a white Honda Insight. I added the license plate number to my notes, folded up the sheet of paper, and tucked it into my shirt pocket. Yeah, the Monarch assignment was over. In common parlance it was a win-win. A win for Wiggin's team and the investors. A big win for whoever took the project. For me, it wasn't a win. I shouldn't have taken it personally, but I did.

As much as the Golden Dragons kept returning to the top of my suspect list, my mind kept returning to Forrester. The Stone Creek Saviors were in the middle of all this somehow, some way. The bloody SCS on the wall at Chan's house and the SCS on the signature line of the ransom note kept pointing to the Saviors. My first encounter with Forrester, his evasiveness, his defiance, and his overall prickliness raised my hackles. He'd not admitted to being a member of the Stone Creek Saviors. Nor had he denied it. A twenty-million-dollar score could fund a lot of eco-terrorism. That thought, and having Forrestor think he one-upped all of us, gnawed at me.

At seven-fifteen, I pulled to the side of the road, a few feet from the entrance to Granderson University, where I could see the administration building and two of the cars marked "Granderson Security." Langford had warned me to stay off campus. I didn't fear him, or even believe he would try to arrest me for trespassing, but avoidance still seemed a more prudent path than flaunting my presence. I turned left, away from the administration building towards the Social Science Building.

The online class schedule had shown Forrester taught an eight o'clock class, followed by another class at ten. As I hoped, he had arrived on campus early for the first class, his Honda sitting in the parking spot closest to the building. I pulled into the space next to it. The rain had turned to a slight drizzle, but it was enough to drive indoors anybody who might be on campus at this hour. As far as I could tell, no one observed me sticking the GPS to the underside of Forrester's car. It was one of the devices left over from the Monarch drop; I hoped the damn thing might be useful this time. I returned to my car and fired up the app to see the GPS signal coming in strong and clear.

If Forrester decided to return home early, I would know it and be able to clear out of his house in plenty of time. I didn't know what I might find there. The perfect scenario would be twenty million dollars in cash and a photo of Forrester standing next to it with a sign reading "Money from the Monarch Project." I held little hope for that. But if I got lucky, I might just find the money.

The rain picked up again as I drove off campus. By now the commute traffic had become heavy. Progress was slow on the back-country roads. The drive from Granderson took me past Folsom Lake, Folsom Prison, the town of Cameron Park, and to the tiny town of Rescue, whose "downtown" consisted of a post office, fire station, two churches, a restaurant, and a community center.

My cell phone trilled: Granderson University. As soon as I answered, Jerry Langford started blistering me.

"Someone said they saw you on campus a few minutes ago. Is that true?"

"Maybe."

"What part about not setting foot on campus ever again do you not understand?"

"Jerry, calm down. I want to apologize for not clueing you in on what was going on with Wiggin and his team. Even though they told me not to tell anybody, I should have kept you in the loop. I'm sorry for—"

"It's a little late for apologies."

"Maybe so, but—"

"Maybe so, nothing. Just stay off campus."

Jerk. "Hey, I forgot to give you the address to send my check."

"What check?"

"For services rendered," I said.

"For services rendered? I ought to sue your ass for breach of contract."

"You hired me to find out what was going on over at Sieboldt with an 'alleged' missing project. I did that. And I helped get the thing returned. Mission accomplished. So you can send my check to—"

He hung up on me. I made a mental note to take Granderson University off my holiday card mailing list.

About a mile past town, I turned onto a country road that climbed and twisted past a couple of horse and sheep ranches. As I continued on, the trees and brush along the side of the road thickened until it seemed I was driving in a narrow tunnel. Ten minutes later, my GPS delivered me to a spot on the road with no visible homes or other structures, just curtains of thick foliage. I cursed the thing, believing the drive across the foothills had been for nothing. Ahead about a hundred feet there appeared to be a clearing in the road where I could turn around and head back down the hill. At the clearing, I noticed a beat-up old mailbox, canted to one side, a boulder propped against it to keep it from falling altogether. The clearing turned out to be a gravel road swathed in even thicker brush. I stepped out into the mist to see if there was a name or address on the mailbox. If there had been it had since rusted over. Inside the box there were no letters or other items to identify the owner or even if the thing was in current use.

I returned to the car and eased up the narrow road, branches from the trees and shrubs scraping against the side of my car as I advanced. Deep puddles dotted the road, and at one point I stopped to ponder whether my car could make it past one particularly deep hole stretching across the width of the road. I gave it a shot, my car slogging through with flying colors. A few hundred feet farther, the vegetation cleared, though the ruts became deeper and more frequent. A couple of the deeper ruts rattled my teeth as I traversed them. When I arrived at a house a little over a mile into the journey, I took a deep breath, relieved I'd made it intact.

The brown, single-story ranch house's most prominent feature was the attached garage comprising a third of the overall structure. The front door was positioned next to the garage, dwarfed by its scale. As I got out of my car to get a better look, the home appeared to be wider than it was deep. Perhaps because the wide front had only two small windows, or maybe it was the lack of landscaping, but something gave the house an inhospitable appearance. I climbed the cement steps onto the porch and knocked on the door. No one answered. I couldn't find a doorbell, so I knocked again, louder this time. While I waited for someone to answer, I pulled out my cell phone and was relieved to see

I still had a cell signal. The GPS app showed Forrester's car remained at Granderson.

When no one came to the door with a plate of cookies or a shotgun leveled at my head, I figured it was safe to give it a go. The front door was locked. I walked around to the back of the unfenced yard. There were no other homes within sight of where I stood, distance and big stands of oak trees providing complete privacy. The plain wooden door in the back was also locked. I took out the lock pick Rubia had given me months before. I'd protested at the time that I wouldn't ever need the thing. She argued she was tired of always doing my dirty work and insisted I take the pick.

I lacked the skill she had with the pick but kept at it, recalling the tips she'd given me. A few missed tries and several curses later, the door swung open, and I stuck my head inside, waiting for an alarm or a dog to respond to my intrusion. Thirty seconds later, I walked in, closing the door behind me.

Before I did anything, I needed to confirm the house I'd broken into was indeed Riley Forrester's. The living room looked like a graduate student's with garage-sale-quality furniture, threadbare and mismatched. On the coffee table was a stack of magazines and publications, including several copies of the *Journal of Sociology* and *American Journal of Sociology*. At the bottom of the stack were three back issues of a magazine called *The Ecologist* with Riley Forrester's name on the mailing label. Bingo. As I was about to set the magazine down, a thought occurred to me. I leafed through *The Ecologist* but didn't find what I'd hoped. I looked through the rest of the magazines on the table. Again, nothing. If Forrester had created the notes used to direct me to the ransom drop site, he'd not cut the letters from any of these magazines.

The floors were hardwood, scraped, and battered, badly in need of refinishing. I checked under the throw rug beneath the coffee table, under the sofa, and under two of the larger chairs, looking for cutouts that might open into a hiding spot beneath the house. I did the same in the kitchen and then looked for any access points to the attic, finding one in a hallway closet. Pulling over a kitchen stool, I pushed aside the flimsy panel covering the square entrance to the attic. My phone's flashlight app provided plenty of light to confirm the only thing in Forrester's attic was a sea of pink insulation and silver ducting.

The house's layout was a simple rectangle, with a kitchen in front, the living room and dining area behind that, and a short hallway where I found three bedrooms and a hallway bath. The first bedroom contained a desk and several bookshelves filled with sociology-themed books and journals. There wasn't a computer, though I did see a power cord and a cable leading to a printer on a side table. Forrester must have owned a laptop and had brought it with him to school. I riffled through the three-drawer file cabinet, finding nothing more than syllabi, handouts for courses he taught, and some bills. There were no under-floor storage spaces, and the closet held nothing but a bunch of junk.

The second bedroom looked like a guest room, though the un-covered mattress plopped on the ground next to a few cinderblocks serving as a nightstand did not provide a welcoming vibe. Forrester's bedroom was slightly warmer, with an unmade bed, a pair of cheap nightstands, and a pinewood dresser. Forrester didn't appear to care much for art or ornamentation, as the only artwork in the entire house was a framed poster featuring the black and white image of a Native American man. Around the man's head circled the words "Man Belongs To The Earth—The Earth Does Not Belong To Man."

On my way back to the kitchen, I glanced at the cluttered dining room table, papers scattered across it from one end to the other. I picked up a sheet of paper containing an aerial Google Earth view of Nimbus Dam. Three red X marks on the photo clustered on one end of the dam. Amid the mix of papers, I found several more photos of the dam from the front, back, side, and aerial perspectives. I leafed through the rest of the papers but found nothing more than printouts from a paper Forrester appeared to be working on regarding social injustice and poverty.

A door from the kitchen led to the garage, where I switched on a light and found a gutted body and frame of a Porsche Carrera. Stacked beside it were several car batteries. On the far side of the garage stood a large workbench. The first thing I noticed was a book, its cover torn and grimy, entitled *How to Build Your Own Electric Vehicle*. Next to that, I saw something more troubling.

Bundled together were six nine-inch cylinders I assumed to be dynamite. A circuit board with a digital clock display had been affixed to the bundle, wires running from it to the two ends of the cylinder in the middle of the bundle. Beside it sat two identical bundles. Three bundles in total, each with six sticks of dynamite. It didn't take a munitions expert to determine eighteen sticks of dynamite could do some serious damage.

twenty-five

I SAT AT THE BAR at seven o'clock that evening watching Rubia and her new bartender Kenny schlepp drinks to the thirty or so patrons crowding the modest confines of the Say Hey, the bar she'd inherited from her uncle a few years before. Five hundred square feet at most, the place featured 453 photographs her uncle, a *Sacramento Bee* photographer, had taken of Willie ("The Say Hey Kid") Mays, an *homage* inspiring the bar's name. I often helped her behind the bar, but she'd insisted on hiring Kenny Hayashi, a twenty-three-year-old law student at the University of Pacific. He was a better bartender than I'd ever been, so I salved my bruised ego by doing my best on the drinking side of the bar.

Benzer hadn't returned any of my calls, nor had he been at his apartment or office when I tried them mid-afternoon. I needed to talk to him. I had a hunch Benzer knew more than he was letting on. About Monarch. And about Thomas Chan. At the same time, I feared for his safety. If Wu and Bo were still on the loose, they would not be happy. They'd be looking for Benzer. And once they found out my identity, they'd come calling on me.

"You worried about the Golden Dragons finding you?" Rubia asked, reading my doleful expression. I'd told her all about the encounter with Wu and Bo.

"Yes. And I'm pissed Trujillo isn't returning any of my calls. I don't know if Benzer and I are out of the woods from those two goons or if they're still at large. It's frustrating. Any ideas?"

"Yeah, don't get shot."

"Any ideas better than that?"

"Keep trying Trujillo."

I glanced at my cell phone on the bar.

"You want another beer?" Rubia asked.

"No thanks."

"You're taking up some good bar space not drinking."

"I'll give you a big tip to make up for it."

"For real, you've been here over an hour, and that's your first beer. What's wrong?"

"Nothing, I just may need to go to work." I held up the phone. I'd been watching the GPS app showing Forrester to be at his home in Rescue, where'd he'd been since returning from Granderson after noon. The fact Forrester appeared to be planning to blow up Nimbus Dam was troubling enough. Just as troubling was its implication regarding the Monarch extortion. Would someone who'd recently hatched a successful twenty-million-dollar scheme want to risk a terrorist attack within a couple of days? That seemed unlikely to me, further obfuscating who might be the culprit.

Not finding the money, or any connection to it at Forrester's house, also bothered me. After I finished searching his house, I'd scoured his property looking for a storage shed or some other place he could have hidden the money and found nothing. If the money was stored offsite, he might lead me to it, thanks to the GPS.

Thirty minutes later, the crowd thinned. I finished the last of my beer, took a final look at my cell, and stuffed it in my pocket. Before I stepped off the barstool to leave, my phone vibrated in my pocket, signaling either a text message or movement on my GPS tracker. Sure enough, my phone showed Riley Forrester was leaving his house.

"Hey," I said to Rubia. "You want to kill an hour with me?"

She was drying glasses and restacking them on a shelf at the back of the bar. She took a quick look around the room, shrugged her shoulders, and said why not. She asked Kenny to cover the bar for the next couple of hours, and then we were out the door and in my car.

"Where we going?" she asked as I turned left off Broadway onto the ramp and merged onto Highway 50.

"Not sure." I handed her my phone. "Follow the little red dot for me, and tell me where it's heading."

She took the phone and scanned the screen. "Who's the red dot?"

"Guy's name is Riley Forrester. He's a sociology professor at Granderson." I proceeded to tell her everything I knew about him, up to and including the map and photos of Nimbus Dam and the three bundles of dynamite I'd found in his home earlier in the day.

"That's some serious shit, professor. Think he's heading there now? To the dam?"

"You tell me."

She looked back at the screen. "He might be."

"Then that's where we're going, too." We were a little farther away from Nimbus Dam than Forrester, but he'd be driving country roads while we could eat up most of the distance by freeway. Traffic was light, so I bumped my speed to about seventy-five in hopes I might be able to beat Forrester to the dam.

"Shouldn't you call the cops?" Rubia asked.

"I called the FBI this morning. Told them about Forrester, the dynamite, the drawings of the dam, and that he might be the Stone Creek Saviors."

"What'd they say?"

"Not much. They listened and said they'd look into it. But I didn't get the sense they were going to drop everything and arrest him."

"Hell, probably have about nine miles of red tape before they'd do that."

I nodded. "Didn't help I called anonymously from a pay phone."

"What's a pay phone?"

"I found one on Florin Road. Even more surprising, it actually worked."

"Why'd you call anonymously?"

"For one thing, I'd have to explain how I happened to be inside Forrester's house."

"There's that."

"Then, they'd want to interview me. My association with Granderson would come up and open the Monarch can of worms. I don't want to go there."

"Should you call the cops now?"

"Let's wait and see if Forrester is going to the dam and if he's planning something tonight. If so, we call them." I held out some hope Forrester might be going to the money, where we could get the drop on him and get it all back.

I exited the freeway at Hazel and turned right on Gold Country Boulevard, the street leading to the parking lot for the Sacramento State University Aquatics Center. As we drove past the south end of the dam, I noticed a tall fence topped with razor wire protected it from entry. I assumed it would be as difficult to access from the north end of the dam as well. A sliver of moon bounced a tiny bit of light off the reservoir's smooth surface. The dam stretched maybe three football fields in length, separating the reservoir from the American River, which sat about fifteen feet below the top of the dam.

I counted fifteen cars in the parking lot, a high number given the hour. Across the lot, light shone through the windows of the second story of the large boathouse. In addition to being a recreational facility for students who wanted to rent kayaks or other self-propelled water-craft, Lake Natoma Reservoir was the home course and training center for the Sac State men and women's rowing teams. I figured the cars belonged to team members who were attending a meeting or training in the boathouse. I was glad to see them so my car wouldn't stand out in what could have been an empty lot.

"Where's Forrester now?"

Rubia enlarged the GPS screen so she could see more detail. "Should be here any second now."

We watched the road leading into the parking lot, anticipating headlights.

"Wait a sec," she said. "He turned off. At the road before Gold Country."

We got out of the car and walked a couple hundred feet past the boathouse, where a finger of water separated us from what appeared to be another parking lot. Unlike ours, the lot across the water was empty. A few seconds later, a car entered and parked in a spot near the water.

"That's him," Rubia said, pointing at the GPS screen.

I got out my binoculars. I hadn't noticed any mounting on Forrester's car earlier in the day, but he now had a kayak strapped to its top. He wore black clothing. As he unstrapped the vessel, a second figure—also in black—exited the passenger side of the car and helped.

Once they rolled the kayak from the roof, the two of them jogged with it towards the water, Forrester in front, the second figure in back. Their movements were so synchronized and efficient, I suspected they'd done this before. Neither of them wore a backpack or carried any other objects I could see.

"You thinking of calling the cops?"

"No. I think it's a practice run," I said. "I don't see any signs of the explosives. If I call the police now, the most it would do is scare them off. Then they'd come back again. Let's just see what they're up to."

A few seconds later, the kayak glided across the water, the slice of moon providing enough light for us to observe their progress. The kayak headed northwest towards the far end of the dam, where the hydroelectric generating equipment had been built. I'd done a little research on the dam earlier in the day, learning it was part of the Central Valley Project, built by the federal government in 1955 for flood control, electrical generation, and recreation in the lake created by the dam. When the water from the lake passed through two turbines within the dam, generating power, it plunged into the American River, which flowed through Sacramento and merged with the Sacramento River. I doubted blowing up the Nimbus Dam would flood Sacramento, but it would cause considerable havoc and be a significant coup for the Stone Creek Saviors.

"What's your big plan now, professor?"

"We have time to get closer to them. Let's walk down the bike trail over to their parking lot and hide closer to Forrester's car."

We walked around the other side of the boathouse and found the bike trail. Once we reached the parking lot, we went to the water's edge. From there I could see the two men as they reached the dam. A few seconds later, a flashlight beam lit the inside of one of the cave-like water inlets underneath the electrical transmission tower at the far end of the wide dam.

"My guess is they're confirming where to put the dynamite," I said.

"When d'you think they'll do it for real? With the dynamite?"

I looked up at the moon and asked Rubia to hand me my phone. Within a minute, I had learned the next day would be a new moon, a night when it wouldn't be visible from earth, the darkest night of the month.

"They're going to do it tomorrow," I said.

"What you going to do about that?"

"I've got to stop them. Just not sure how yet."

We moved behind a stand of trees and thick underbrush no more than fifteen feet from Forrester's car. It was peaceful out there in the dark by the lake, a nice contrast to all I'd been through the previous few days. The night was refreshingly cool, the kind of evening where your cheeks turned red and your soul felt invigorated. Before I let myself get too transcendental, I reminded myself we were observing two probable felons practicing their plan to blow up federal property.

"Have you found out anything more about the Golden Dragons?" I asked.

"Still waiting on my guy in LA."

"Ask him if he knows anything more about this Wu Wing guy who owns the Camaro. And his sidekick, Bo. He was younger and smaller."

"Still can't believe you *Training Day*'d those two."

"Yeah." I held up a hand to quiet her. "Hold on, I see them at the shoreline."

It had taken a long time for them to complete their reconnaissance and row back towards their car. Returning to shore, the two men were as efficient as they'd been during their departure from car to dam, jogging in unison with the boat between them. Without a word, they placed the kayak upside down on top of the car and secured it. I could make out Forrester's face framed with a black beanie and turtleneck. The other man's back was to me.

"What's your watch say?" the man asked.

"Twenty-two minutes," Forrester said.

"That's good, isn't it?"

"Yeah, Seth, it is. Let's go."

Moments later they got in the car and drove off.

Seth. Seth Seeger. The snotty student who'd turned his nose up at the beer I'd bought him. The president of Students Saving Our Planet, S-SOP. And now, it appeared, co-conspirator in a plot to blow up a dam.

twenty-six

FIRST THING IN THE MORNING, I tried Benzer's cell and office phones yet again. Then I drove to his apartment and office, finding both locked and dark. Either he'd gone to ground or the Golden Dragons had gotten to him. I left yet another voice message for Lieutenant Trujillo asking him if he had followed up on my initial call and paid a visit to my friends Wu and Bo. If not, Benzer might never be found, at least not alive. I'd not heard anything in the news about Sac PD arresting them or any updates on Chan's murder. Everything pointed to the Asian gangsters as the killers. But something about Forrester still bugged me, the bloody "SCS" scrawled on Chan's wall still vivid in my mind.

Under threatening skies I parked two blocks off campus, keeping an eye out for Granderson security as I approached the school. At nine forty in the morning, I entered the Social Science Building, where Riley Forrester was teaching an "Introduction to Sociology" class. I peered in through the vertical sliver of window on a door at the back of the room. About thirty students filled about a third of a theatre-style lecture hall. Ten minutes remained in the class period, so I eased open the door and took a seat in the back.

Forrester stood at a lectern maybe forty feet away. The seats sloped down from back to front, so the professor stood where the rest of the students and I looked down on him. If he noticed me, he gave no sign of it.

"Marx belonged to a radical group of scholars known as the He-gelians, named after the philosopher George Hegel from the late eighteenth and early nineteenth century." Forrester lectured without use of accompanying slides, glancing at his notes as he spoke. "Over time, Marx broke away from this dialectic philosophy and concluded alienation from society comes from material conditions, not from thought, as the Hegelians theorized. Marx advocated changing the conditions of society to reduce alienation by the populace. He predict-ed the revolutions by the working class that occurred in nineteenth century Europe."

At least five students had nodded off at this point of the lecture. Two others on the other side of the room were engaged in a hushed conversation.

"His ideas were considered radical at the time, and he was forced to move from city to city all over Europe," Forrester continued. "So you see, just as it is today, progressive thinkers are considered danger-ous. They, and their ideas, are seen as radical, but in the end, it is radical thinkers—and more importantly, radical *doers*—who move society forward."

A young woman in the center of the lecture hall raised her hand, and Forrester pointed at her.

"Are you saying the revolutionaries and terrorists are what make a society better?"

"That's precisely what I'm saying."

The statement caused a buzz in the room, even two of the sleep-ing students awoke and tuned in. "What if the aims of the terrorists are to tear down society?" a young man two rows in front of me asked.

"Define 'tear down,'" the professor said, making air quotes with his fingers.

"To destroy property," the student shot back. "To kill innocent people."

"I maintain there is no such thing as 'innocent people.'" Again with the air quotes. "There are those who perpetuate the ills of society actively and those who do so passively by not paying attention to the evils their society promotes."

The student started to reply, then stopped himself and shook his head.

"Any other questions?" Forrester asked, more of a challenge than a request for more inquiries. When no one raised a hand, he took off his glasses and looked around the classroom. "Next time, we'll pick up with Marx and his view of capitalism. Make sure you read chapter nine before the next class."

I remained seated in the back as the students gathered their notebooks and stuck them into their backpacks. Several of them paused to check their cell phones for text messages. Two female students approached Forrester after class and engaged him in short conversations. When the second young woman finished her conversation with the professor, she walked up the aisle past me and out the back door.

Forrester was stuffing his lecture notes into a briefcase. "May I ask what you're doing here?" He didn't bother to look up at me.

"Learning about Karl Marx."

"Buy a book and read about him. This class is for students only. Not old farts like you."

"Old fart? I admit to being in the summer of my life. But an old fart? I'm insulted. Besides, I'm a former college professor myself. I'd think you could extend me at least a modicum of professional courtesy." I gave him a sweet smile.

He finished with his briefcase and strode up the aisle towards me, stopping as he reached the end of the row where I sat. He set his briefcase on a desktop, though he kept his hand on its handle.

"Believe me," he said, pointing a finger at me. "I am being courteous. You wouldn't like what discourteous looks like."

"For a sociology professor you have a tough time relating to others. Maybe you should consider a new line of work. You were pretty good with that pitchfork the other day. A more agrarian line of work might suit you better."

"I asked you why you're here."

"So you did." I stood up from the desk and looked at him a few seconds before continuing. "I don't even know where to start. But let's try this. Tell me where you put the twenty million dollars you stole."

He looked at me impassively, unmoved by what I'd said. "Twenty million. You think I'd be standing in a lecture hall at nine in the morning dispensing information to a bunch of over-privileged nineteen-year-olds if I had twenty million dollars?"

"What about the psychic rewards of the profession?"

"Psychic rewards. That's good. No, really, what are you talking about? Twenty million dollars."

"I can see you're not going to tell me anything about the money, so let's move the conversation along."

"Let's."

"I asked you about Thomas Chan last time, and you walked away. What I want to know is why an eco-terrorist group like the Stone Creek Saviors would want to kill a young business man."

"How the hell would I know?" Chan's name brought no discernable reaction to Forrester's demeanor.

"You're a scholar with considerable research interest in environmental activism. I would think you'd have some idea why the Saviors took credit for killing Chan."

"What makes you think they took credit for killing him?"

It occurred to me the police hadn't released details from the Chan murder scene, including the "SCS" written in blood on his wall. "Let's say they did, for the sake of argument."

"It's a ludicrous argument. I'm not going to speculate on something that's patently untrue."

"Would it surprise you to know Chan told me he'd received threatening messages from someone saying they were the Saviors? They didn't like him doing business with companies over in China because they're among the biggest polluters on the planet."

"If he was doing business with the Chinese, then no, it wouldn't surprise me an environmental group would be upset with him. Doesn't mean they'd kill him."

I looked for signs of nerves as he spoke, anything that might reveal if he was lying or not. In my two encounters with the man, I'd become convinced he was a liar, a practiced and accomplished one. I wouldn't be able to trip him up with wordplay or verbal bullying. As much as I disagreed with his ideology of violent methods justifying social ends, I had to say Forrester was a man steadfast in his beliefs.

"You'd better not go through with your plan to blow up Nimbus Dam."

This time he did blink, and his face colored. He shifted his weight from one foot to the other.

"You may think you're doing society a great service, awakening the impassive masses, or whatever misguided theories you operate under, but blowing up a dam and firebombing an academic building is nothing less than a cowardly, criminal act. So I'm warning you to stop now."

"You're warning me? Who the fuck are you to warn me about anything? I don't know what you think you know, or how you came to think it, but to come into my classroom and accuse me of terrorism is the height of insolence. I should call campus security."

I wanted to tell him about the dynamite I found at his home and watching him and Seeger's dry run the night before, but I didn't want to reveal myself. Leaving him wondering how I knew about his plans gave me an upper hand I didn't want to relinquish.

"It's bad enough you're planning to blow up the dam, but to involve a student in your scheme is horrific. You have no right to involve a kid in something that could ruin the rest of his life."

"I have no idea what or who you are talking about."

"Seth Seeger."

Again, he blinked and shifted his weight.

"Did you help him set up S-SOP as sort of a minor league team for your Stone Creek Saviors? Kind of like a development squad so you could teach him the fine art of bomb making and radical rhetoric?"

"I'm not sure what world you're living in," he said, picking up his briefcase. "But it sure as hell isn't connected to reality."

"I'm warning you. If you try to go through with your plot, I will stop you." I moved down the row of seats until I was less than two feet from him. "I've already called the FBI. If the dam blows, they'll know who did it."

"You're out of your mind." His voice lacked its usual defiance.

"Don't test me on this."

"If I was going to blow up Nimbus Dam like you said, how in the hell would you stop me?"

I didn't know the answer to his question. I'd hoped telling him what I knew would stop him. If it didn't, I would need to go to Plan B, whatever the hell that was.

twenty-seven

FULTON AVENUE WAS SACRAMENTO'S "Auto Row," home to most of the major automobile retailers in the area. All three of Danny's dealerships resided on Fulton within one mile of each other. Cashmore Lexus was his crown jewel, the one he'd battled three ex-wives to retain. I met him on the showroom floor. My car was getting long on miles, and Danny promised me a deal if I was interested in a Lexus.

"This one's loaded, of course, so it's a bit over your budget," he said. "But I could knock five grand off the price if you really want it."

He was right. The RCS 350 was about ten grand more than I wanted to spend. I'd never been much of a car guy, but this thing was gorgeous, loaded with luxury and safety features I'd never considered before, but which now seemed required in my next car. The new car smell was intoxicating, and I took in a big breath of it as I grasped the polished wood steering wheel.

"Man, the chicks would go crazy for a good-looking guy like you driving this thing."

"I'm fifty-two years old," I said. "There's not a lot of 'chicks' in my life, let alone ones going crazy over me."

"This baby could jump start your world, Ray."

"I can see why you've made millions selling cars. It's not about the machines. It's about the ego. Especially when it comes down to sex."

He laughed. "The formula's worked for thirty years. No reason to change now."

"I wouldn't mind test driving one of these, even if you are manipulating the hell out of me."

Danny had called me to ask if I'd completed my investigation of Jolene. I tried to stall by saying I needed to double-check a few facts, hoping in the meantime Jolene would break up with him. But he insisted on learning what I had so far. Now I didn't want to go through with it. I wanted to keep talking cars to avoid the inevitable awkward conversation about his girlfriend.

"So?" he said. "Are you ready to spill or what?"

"What?"

"Your report on Jolene. What did you find out?"

"Well…so how close are you to popping the question to this woman?" My report on Jolene? What did I want to tell him? She was a good kisser? She was planning on breaking up with him?

He pulled out a ring box from his jacket pocket, opening it to reveal an engagement ring with a diamond that had to be three carats. "She and I are having dinner tomorrow at The Kitchen. If you give me the green light today, then that's when I'm springing this on her."

I climbed out of the car and shut the door with a solid thump. Danny and I stood face to face. "You sure she feels the same way you do? No offense, Danny, but sometimes you can be a bit impulsive. I mean, you married your first wife because her dad said he'd give you his '57 Chevy."

"What a sweet car."

"But Sherry not so much."

"Not a match made in heaven, no," he said.

"Maybe you should take things slower, just to be sure. You know, give it some time."

"Ray, thanks for looking out for me. But I'm the same age as you. We've both been around the block two or three times. I'm not entering this relationship blind. I can also tell when a woman is into me. I think she and I are right for each other."

"What kind of mileage does a car like this get?" I turned towards the car.

"Like the sticker right in front of you says. Mid-twenties overall between freeway and city driving. Why are you stalling me? Did you find something about Jolene?"

"No. Everything checked out fine. Her work history has been great. Credit scores are above solid. Owns her home with good equity. The whole nine yards. You knew she'd been married, right?"

"Yeah, of course. Her husband died years ago."

I opened the door to the car and stuck my head inside to get another whiff of the new leather seats. I knew the right thing to do was to wait for Jolene to tell Danny herself the relationship was ending, but Danny was leaving me little choice. I needed to tell him his feelings for Jolene were not reciprocated. It wouldn't be pleasant, but he needed to know the truth. I already made up my mind not to see her again, even though I wanted to. It wouldn't be right. And if I did date her, how would it look if she and I ran into Danny? No, Danny was a friend, and even if I could justify dating Jolene after she broke up with him, I wouldn't feel good about it. Jolene and I were not going to happen. Unfortunately, neither were Danny and Jolene. I took a deep breath and prepared to tell him exactly that. As I was about to pull my head out of the car, I heard Danny's voice boom.

"Baby! What a great surprise!"

"I came to give you a little treat. I know how much you love the desserts from Rick's, so I thought I'd bring you something. I thought maybe we could talk, too. I need to tell you something." It was Jolene.

Keeping my head stuck inside the car for the duration of her visit was not an option. Neither was climbing in the driver's seat, closing the door, and locking it. I backed my head out of the car and shut the door. I could feel my face reddening before she and I even made eye contact.

"Jolene, I'd like you to meet one of my best friends," Danny said. "We go all the way back to college. This is Ray Courage."

I stood there speechless, busted, my face a mask of shame. The color drained from her face the second she saw me. Her mouth double-clutched as she tried to process the situation in front of her and come up with the appropriate response. Then a calm crossed her face, as if she just then comprehended how Danny, she, and I found ourselves together.

"I believe we've already met," she said.

"Yes, we have." We didn't go through the charade of shaking hands there in front of Danny.

"You've met?"

"I was going to let you know, Danny," I said.

"Let him know what? That you came to Sacramento Oaks to spy on me? That we had lunch together?"

"It's not like that," I said, though it was like that.

"I should have put it together once I learned you were a private eye. You lying low-life. How dare you lead me on when it was all in a day's work for you. Were you in it for the sport, or was it to show up Danny?"

"Look, this is a bit complicated," I said.

"I'm not sure I understand what's going on," Danny said.

"Goddamn, Danny, you prick. I can tell you what's going on. You hired one of your quote-unquote best friends to look into me, to see if I was worthy of your companionship. I'm not sure what your plans were, but what are you afraid of? Did you think I was going to marry you like your other bimbos and then take over one of your fucking car dealerships?"

For the first time I can remember, Danny's face grew red and he was speechless. "What did he do to make you so angry, Jolene?"

"Jolene," I said, hoping against hope to save this moment. "Danny did hire me. But it was purely precautionary. He's told me how much he cares about you. You have to understand, in his situation he has to be careful. Please try to understand."

"Jolene, I'm sorry—" Danny started.

"Did you tell him I asked you out to lunch?" Jolene asked, turning to me. "Did you tell him that?"

"No. To be honest, I wasn't sure how to work it into my report."

"She asked you out?"

I gave him a pained look.

"Yeah, I asked him out. And we had a nice lunch. A couple of drinks. A nice hot kiss. How do you feel about that, Danny? Are you angry? Does it make you feel justified in sending a private eye snooping after me?"

"What did you do to make her ask you out?" Danny asked me.

"Be my usual charming self?" The attempt at humor fell flat in the auto showroom.

"Did you fucking hit on her?"

"Not as far as I know."

"You arrogant son of a bitch," she said. "You had been flirting with me all morning at the country club. You didn't have the balls to ask me out when we were saying goodbye, so you left me little choice but to do it myself."

"And you kissed her, Ray?"

I gave him a slight nod.

"Well, this is all wonderful news," Danny said. "My girlfriend turns out to be a two-timing slut, and my friend turns out to be a backstabbing horn dog. Great, just great. Ray, you can forget about a deal on the car."

Danny stormed off the showroom floor for parts unknown. Without even a parting dirty look, Jolene hustled off in the other direction, leaving me alone with the Lexus and the knowledge I was the biggest jerk in Sacramento.

twenty-eight

THE LUNCH DANNY AND I had planned after our meeting in the Lexus showroom never happened once he decided to disown me as a friend. Lacking a lunch companion and an appetite, I left earlier than planned for Cache Creek, an Indian casino about forty-five miles west of Sacramento. The drive gave me ample time to reflect on the past few days, though I had trouble getting past the day's most recent events. How had I managed to alienate a smart, beautiful woman who had been attracted to me, while destroying a thirty-year friendship with a man I would do anything for? I wanted to make things right with both of them but feared I had damaged both relationships beyond repair. Even worse, I had ruined *their* relationship. Even if Jolene had planned to break it off with Danny, the two might have maintained a friendship. They might even have worked things out. Now, thanks to me, those prospects seemed remote at best.

Once I drove past Davis, the route became one rural country road after another as I traversed almond and walnut orchards, horse ranches, sheep ranches, and monotonous wide-open spaces. Cache Creek Casino had become a destination resort about ten years before, with a world-class golf course, weekend entertainment headliners rivaling those in San Francisco, and a hotel and three-star restaurant drawing people from hundreds of miles away.

I parked on the fifth level of the high-rise garage and walked to the elevator. The first thing to hit me when I exited the elevator onto the casino floor was the smoke. The noxious fumes of cigarettes caused me to cough and put a palm over my nose. California's indoor spaces had long ago become smoke-free; Indian land had its own sovereignty, meaning they had the right to set their own smoking laws. Gamblers tended to be smokers. Indian casinos needed gamblers. End of story.

For mid-week, mid-afternoon, the crowd was larger than expected, consisting mainly of older Asian men and women, many of whom had no doubt been transported by the several tour buses I noticed parked in front of the casino. A steady racket filled the cavernous room, punctuated now and then by shouts and whoops and the clatter and clang of slot machines. And everywhere, cigarette smoke.

It took about twenty minutes of walking the casino floor to spot Seth Seeger. In a black vest and white shirt, his curly hair tamed by a stout hair product, and his usual truculence quelled by the job, he projected a different image than the young man I'd encountered a few days before. His blackjack table was empty, and he busied himself by examining the six-inch stack of cards in front of him.

"Hello, Seth," I said, settling into a seat opposite him at the blackjack table.

He didn't seem to know who I was at first. But when recognition sank in, his face darkened. "What do you want?"

"Nice to see you, too."

"How did you know I worked here?"

"A friend of mine has a Facebook account and looked you up. You know, if you're planning on a career in eco-terrorism you might want to rethink your relationship with social media."

"Very funny."

"Aren't you going to deal me a hand?" I dropped fifty dollars worth of chips on the table in front of me.

Seth looked up at a spot above and behind me. I followed his gaze to a smoked plexiglass sphere mounted to the tall ceiling, no doubt security cameras watching every move of gamblers and dealers alike. With his bosses watching, Seth had no choice but to play cards with me.

I anted in five bucks. He dealt our cards. I had a ten of spades and a seven of clubs. He had a blackjack. Game over.

"It's your lucky day," I said as he collected my five dollars in chips.

"I get paid the same whether I win or lose."

"This seems like an interesting job for someone of your persuasion," I said.

"What do you mean? My persuasion?"

"I don't know. You're a socially conscious young man. Not that there's anything wrong with gambling, per se, but I'd have thought you'd be working at a soup kitchen, building solar box cookers, or petitioning to save the whales."

He ignored me and dealt the next hand. I was glad no one else sat at the table because I wanted to talk to Seth, but also because I didn't know much about playing blackjack other than the goal was to get as close to twenty-one as possible without going over. I knew there were strategies for doubling down, splitting cards, and so on, but I didn't have a clue about any of that. This time my cards totaled fourteen. "I'll hold," I said.

His cards totaled seventeen, which I read on the rule board on my way in meant he had to hit if it was a "soft" seventeen, meaning one of the cards was an ace. He drew a six of hearts, which with his six of spades and ace of clubs gave him thirteen. He hit again and drew a queen of hearts, putting him over twenty-one. I won back my five dollars.

"I know you didn't come here to play blackjack," he said.

"You're right. I came here to talk about Thomas Chan and the twenty million dollars you stole."

"Thomas Chan? The dude who just got offed? And what are you talking about? Twenty million dollars?"

"You didn't threaten Chan in an e-mail to stop dealing with the Chinese?"

"Maybe I did. Maybe I didn't. Either way I'm not telling you."

I was tired of getting stonewalled by each and every person I'd talked to about Thomas Chan and Monarch. I didn't even have enough to determine if there was a connection between the dead man and the stolen project. I knew Seth Seeger wouldn't help me, so I needed to change directions.

"Let me make this simple." I looked around to make sure no one had drawn within earshot. "Do not go through with you plans at Nimbus Dam."

He started to reach for the next set of cards, but my words stopped him. "I don't know what you're talking about."

"I thought you'd say that. And I'm not going to go back and forth with you about it. I know what you and Forrester have planned, and I'm warning you to stop. I've called the fibbies and given them a detailed description of your entire operation."

"You don't have any idea what you are talking about."

"Even if you don't go forward tonight like you're planning, they'll have eyes on you. If you get anywhere near Nimbus Dam, you'll be arrested."

"For what?"

"For the three little bundles Forrester made." I wasn't sure whether casino security had listening devices in the blackjack pits, so I tried to keep my comments vague.

He didn't say a word for the next three hands as he proceeded to take fifteen bucks from me.

"You're a young man," I said. "I think your idealism is commendable. I do. But there are better ways to act on your ideals than the methods Forrester promotes. He's a criminal, Seth. Don't associate with him. If you want to enact change, do something positive. Lobby your elected officials. Hell, get yourself elected. Write articles about your beliefs. I wasn't kidding before about the petitions. Generate positive energy."

He laughed and shook his head. "You're a piece of work. From what old movie did you get that speech? 'Generate positive energy.' Oh my god." He rolled his eyes and gave a derisive snort.

"Too much soapbox for you, huh?"

"Maybe you should find another table."

"Maybe so." I knew my pep talk would prove futile but figured it was worth a shot. Two and a half decades teaching college students gave me a sense about students who could be reasoned with and those who could not. Seth Seeger had so bought into Forrester's worldview I might just as well have told him the Easter Bunny, Santa Claus, and the Tooth Fairy would be joining us for a round of blackjack. I put my remaining chips into the middle of the table. "One more hand."

He shrugged and started to deal. He threw down my first card before dealing his. He then set down my next card. "Nine of diamonds."

My two cards totaled eleven. I was about to ask for another card, when he laid down his second card, the ace of spades. He peeled back the corner of his down card before declaring, "Blackjack. The house wins." He revealed his down card, a ten of diamonds.

My money all gone, I stood to leave. Seth didn't meet my eye as he collected my money. "Remember that, Seth. The house almost always wins. And I'm not just talking about cards."

"What are you talking about?"

"I'm saying if you plan to go up against the house—the police, government, whatever—don't count on winning."

Outside, it was nice to see daylight and breathe fresh air. The lack of windows inside the casino, accompanied by the sensory overload of noise, smoke, and flashing lights, had given me a headache. I needed a shower and an ibuprofen. A sign indicated the golf course and the employee parking lot were up the hill above the casino. I walked the half-mile to the employee lot.

I figured warning Forrester to terminate his plans to bomb Nimbus Dam had given me away. While he might not have guessed I'd broken into his home and discovered the bombs, he could have reasoned I'd tracked his movements. A quick search under his bumper and he'd have found the GPS transmitter. In that case, I'd need another method to keep tabs on his movements.

It took fifteen minutes to find Seth's car in the vast employee parking lot. I placed a second GPS device from the Monarch drop on the underside of the car and hoped neither Seth nor Forrester would discover it.

twenty-nine

I WAS HOPING FOR HEAVY traffic so I could use it as an excuse for missing my four o'clock appointment with Dr. Nelson. One of his assistants had called me earlier in the day on orders from the doctor insisting I come in for a short meeting. The woman was not specific about why Dr. Nelson wanted to see me, but I had an idea. After my day so far, a conversation with a doctor was low on my list of priorities.

Just my luck, traffic from Cache Creek back to Sacramento was light, and I arrived ten minutes early. Five of us sat in the waiting room for our turn with a doctor, physician's assistant, or nurse practitioner.

The same *Golf Magazine* I'd leafed through during my last visit lay on an end table. My earlier enthusiasm to start up the game again had waned. A glance at the magazine, its cover featuring a lush golf course not unlike Sacramento Oaks, brought back the image of Jolene's incensed face. A wave of embarrassment and disgrace washed over me. I picked up a copy of *Nutrition Weekly* and read how to add kale into my diet, create a fat-burning meal plan, and increase dietary fat to improve regularity. By the time I finished reading the ads for the weight loss getaway vacation in the back of the magazine, I was the only person sitting in the waiting room.

A little after five, Dr. Nelson himself swung open the door to the waiting room and called my name. He shook my hand as I reached the door and apologized for the delay. "We had a lot of late walk-ins, I'm afraid." He stepped back, and I followed him down the hallway.

In all the years I'd been coming to see him, I didn't realize he had an actual office beyond the reception area, the examination rooms, and file room. He shut the door behind us. I sat down in one of the guest chairs as he settled into his desk chair. The office was cozy, the walls decorated with undersea photographs of colorful fish and coral. I knew from the many years of seeing Dr. Nelson that his two hobbies consisted of scuba diving and photography.

He was in his late fifties and his expressions tilted towards somber on a good day. He looked at me with a grim face.

"Can you tell me what's going on?" he asked.

"What do you mean?" I knew what he meant.

"I got a call from Dr. Beckly."

"Oh?"

"He said you didn't show up for your appointment the other day. You didn't call to cancel and haven't returned any of his calls to reschedule. So, that's what I mean when I ask what's going on."

"Oh, that?" I sounded like a teenager whose parents found a bong in his bedroom.

"Ray, I'm concerned about you. When we talked the other day, you described some serious symptoms. Very serious. Severe nightmares. Flashbacks. Anxiety attacks and so on." He reached over and retrieved a folder from the side of his desk. He opened it and read through it, refreshing his memory. "You said you were hyperventilating even. That's not good."

I smiled nervously. What was it about doctors that made an adult act like he was a little kid, his own life experience no match for that of an exalted medical authority? "I've been feeling better."

"Okay. I'm glad to hear that. Have you had any side effects from the Zoloft?" He picked up a pen, poised to add whatever I told him into my file.

"No. No side effects."

"That's good."

"To be honest, I haven't started taking the pills yet."

"What? Why?"

"Like I said, I've been feeling much better."

He exhaled, part frustration with me, part fatigue from the long day. He looked tired, and the last thing he wanted at the end of his day was an uncooperative patient. "Why do you think you're feeling much better?"

"It's kind of hard to explain." I tried to gather my thoughts. I hadn't formed in my own mind the words I needed to tell him. "When

I came in the other day and told you about my symptoms, I probably shouldn't have. I regretted it once I got back home."

"You regretted coming to see your personal physician?" Nelson tossed his pen onto the desk and sat back in his chair.

"Nothing personal. It's not like that. It's just maybe I wasn't as forthcoming as I should have been with my symptoms and all."

I thought back on the images that had prompted me to come see the doctor. The pictures in my head and my reactions to them made me believe something was wrong with me, that I'd gone down an unhealthy path whose final destination might be ruinous. My thoughts and emotions had scared me. That's what had driven my earlier visit. The past couple of days had helped me gain more clarity around those thoughts and emotions than therapy or Zoloft could provide. At least that's what I told myself.

"Care to elaborate?" Dr. Nelson asked.

Did I want to elaborate? Would doing so help me gain further insight into my current state of mind? I took a deep breath and released it. "What's your biggest fear?" I asked the doctor.

"Excuse me?"

"What do you fear more than anything?"

He looked at me long and hard before he spoke. "I'm going to assume this will lead to some sort of explanation about your state of mind. So with that premise in mind, I'll answer your question. I fear getting a terminal disease."

"Of course, we all do. What else, if you were to obsess over it, would keep you from falling to sleep at night?"

Nelson shrugged and outstretched his arms, palms up. "Who knows? Maybe that some harm might come to my loved ones, especially my children."

"Yes." I leaned towards him. "We fear that for a lot of reasons, but two reasons stand out. First, because they are our children, the people we love most. We don't want anything bad to happen to them. Secondly, we feel powerless in protecting them. As much as we love them, as much as we do for them, we can't be there twenty-four hours a day, seven days a week to take care of them and prevent bad things from happening. Even if we could, there's no guarantee we could stop the bad from happening. Am I making sense?"

"I hear what you're saying," he said.

"Once I got married, I obsessed over something bad happening to my wife. When our daughter arrived, my fears got even worse. Now I had two people to worry about. It was on my mind a lot. It wasn't crippling, but it made me feel weak and powerless."

"To a certain extent those are normal human emotions," he said. "Unless these thoughts become too prevalent and you become anxious and fearful all the time."

"For me, I was borderline. I could put my fears aside when I was working or engaged in something, but in my downtime they dominated my thoughts."

"That's not healthy."

"And when my wife was killed, those feelings intensified. It was as if my wife getting killed showed me how powerless I was. And how justified I was to have those fears. My poor daughter became the source of my overprotectiveness."

"From what I know of your daughter, she shows no signs of being harmed by your concerns for her."

"That's because she's a terrific person. In spite of my parenting."

"Where are you going with this?" Nelson asked.

"I told you about the nightmares. And you said you read about what happened."

"Yes."

"And many years before that day, people had hurt my family."

"Go on."

"All of a sudden, my view of things changed. I was no longer fearful of unseen evil. Now I was angry and wanted to do something about it. For the first time in my life I felt I had the power over the bad stuff in the world instead of it having power over me. When I took things into my own hands, it felt good."

"But then later you had some remorse and PTSD set in, correct?"

I shook my head. "I expected that to happen. Especially when I had the nightmares. But even though the nightmares were frightening, I always woke up with a sense of newfound power. I felt good. Even when the images came to me when I was awake, it was the same thing. I felt empowered."

Dr. Nelson thought for a few seconds. He glanced again at his notes. "Then why did you come to see me complaining of symptoms of PTSD?"

"Good question. I guess it was because I was afraid my feelings weren't normal. I thought maybe they were some form of PTSD. It didn't seem right those violent images stimulated me. All of a sudden I had changed. I was a well-educated, liberal-leaning college professor who advocated peaceful solutions over violence or taking the law into one's hand. Now, when I look in the mirror I see someone who says screw it, if somebody messes with me or someone I love, I'll do whatever it takes to protect us. The transformation scared me. So, I came to see you."

"I don't know what to say." He crossed his arms over his chest and sat back in his chair. "Are you still worried about this?"

"No. I know my outlook now implies a sort of moral high ground, that I've made myself judge, jury, and executioner. That's something I would've condemned before. But those traumatic events gave me an epiphany. I won't be victimized. My family and friends won't be victimized. Not as long as I have a say in the matter."

thirty

RUBIA AND I ARRIVED AT the same parking lot as the night before, again parking near the Sacramento State University Aquatics Center. It was before six in the evening, the sun already set, the lake smooth and tranquil in front of us.

"I'm tired of this place," Rubia said.

"We've been here twice. Get over it."

"Twice in two days is too much."

"Here, this will make you feel better." I reached into the back seat and grabbed a brown paper bag and handed it to her. I picked up a second bag for myself. "Oscar's."

She looked in the bag. "Where's the rest of my food?"

"The rest of your food? There's a breakfast burrito, a carnitas burrito, and a quesadilla. If that's not enough to get you through the evening then we'll order a pizza."

"You know me and my metabolism," she said, already two bites into the quesadilla.

"Yeah, I know. Like a hummingbird."

"Um, hum," she said, her mouth full. "What'd you get?"

"Three taquitos."

"Well, isn't that dainty of you." She finished the quesadilla and unwrapped the breakfast burrito. "I don't see the cops anywhere."

"Not cops. FBI. I think the feds would be insulted if you called them cops. When we drove in, I saw two guys behind the equipment shed that could have been feds. I'm sure there's more of them somewhere." As I finished talking, I could see movement across the lake beyond the transmission tower near the spot Forrester and Seeger visited the night before.

"You call them anonymously again?"

"Yep."

It was a bit early to expect the would-be bombers. If their dry-run was an indication, their operation would start at about eight, after it would have been pitch dark for a couple of hours. Then again, it could happen later. I checked my cell phone and confirmed Seth Seeger's car was still parked at Granderson. Unlike the night before, no other cars were parked in the lot. I started in on my first taquito when a rapping on my side window startled me.

"Can I ask what you're doing here, sir?" He wore a baseball cap and a windbreaker with FBI stenciled on the breast. He did not look happy.

"Just enjoying the lake and having dinner with my friend here."

"I'm afraid you're going to have to leave. This area's closed tonight."

I considered protesting but didn't see the reason. I'd come to prevent Forrester from going through with his plot in case the FBI didn't show up. Now with the FBI on the scene, I wasn't going to do anything but get in the way. "Sure, officer."

We left the lot, and I parked on the side of Hazel Avenue, about a quarter mile away. The spot offered a view of the downstream side the dam, meaning I wouldn't be able to see a kayak approaching on the lake side, but I might be able to see the FBI move into action to make their arrest.

"That was wimpy of you," Rubia said.

"What?"

"'Sure, officer,'" she said in a baby voice.

"I didn't hear you citing the Bill of Rights."

"Well—"

"Hold on," I said as I looked at my cell phone. "Looks like Seeger is leaving Granderson." After his shift at Cache Creek had ended, Seeger had headed to campus about the same time I'd finished with Dr. Nelson. He was now leaving campus.

I set my cell phone in the console between us. Rubia and I watched for about forty minutes as Seth's car headed east, using the same route I'd travelled two days before. The route to Riley Forrester's home in Rescue.

"He must be meeting the professor at his place, then heading over here in one car like last night," I said. "Unfortunately, we won't be able to track them since Forrester found my GPS."

Seeger arrived at Forrester's house a few minutes later and spent more than an hour there. I wondered what they were doing for so long. A little after nine o'clock, Seeger's car was on the move again. Either he was following Forrester, leaving on his own, or Forrester was riding with him. They wound down the country roads until they hit Highway 50 in the direction of Nimbus Dam.

"You think Forrester, Seeger, or both of them killed Chan?" Rubia asked.

"My money's on the Golden Dragons. I think the kid got in over his head with a big loan and couldn't pay them back. They cut off his fingers to show they weren't messing around and then when he couldn't pay the vig they killed him."

"Doesn't make sense. If they kill Chan then he can't pay what he owes."

"No, but Benzer can. I figured they killed Chan to put the fear of god into Benzer and motivate him to find the money any way he can."

"If you think it's the Dragons, then why we dealing with these clowns?" She pointed at my cell phone as I continued to track the car's movement.

"For one thing, because I don't want them to blow up a dam. But I also think it's possible Forrester in particular could have done it. Not sure why he would. Maybe because of Chan's business dealings. SCS warned him about that."

"Or maybe it's all about this Monarch shit. You know, like Chan and SCS both wanted to gank the thing."

"Yeah. Makes my head hurt trying to sort it all out."

Seeger's car approached the Hazel Avenue exit, a busy four-lane thoroughfare. From our position across the street, I doubted I could identify Seeger's car, but I would be able to spot anyone turning onto Gold Country Boulevard towards the Aquatics Center. I took my eyes off the GPS and focused on the incoming traffic on Hazel. At least two dozen cars drove past the exit without turning onto Gold Country. I checked my phone again and was surprised to see the car had not exited at Hazel and was continuing on towards downtown.

"That's weird," I said. "They didn't turn off."

"Maybe they missed the exit."

"Maybe." When they continued past the Sunrise Boulevard exit three miles later, I was convinced they weren't coming back to Nimbus Dam. "We should follow them."

"What if it's just the kid driving to see his girlfriend or something?"

That didn't make sense to me. Seeger had driven all the way from Cache Creek east to Granderson, then even farther east to Forrester's. Now he was driving west in the direction where he'd started from hours ago, in the general direction of Cache Creek Casino. I handed Rubia my phone and started the car. "Tell me where they're going and I'll follow."

We blew through Sacramento about ten minutes behind Seth's car. When they turned north on Highway 113 east of Davis, my GPS app froze.

"Freakin' thing died, Ray."

"Am I getting a cell signal?"

"Not much. One bar."

"Maybe that's the problem. I'll keep going down 113 and see if the reception's better. Try restarting the thing." I didn't want to give up because Seeger was now about two-thirds the way to Cache Creek, an unlikely round-trip. He was up to something. I just knew it.

Rubia turned off my phone and restarted it as I drove. When the screen came back to life, I'd gained one more bar of signal strength, but the GPS app was still worthless. I banged on the steering wheel with both palms, disappointed and frustrated. There was no sense driving aimlessly. I had to admit defeat. At least for tonight. I pulled off at Covell Boulevard to turn around. When we reached the freeway on the way back to Sacramento, the app kicked back in.

"We're good, prof. They stopped somewhere close to Woodland."

"Got an address?"

"They're on County Road 97. Let me see what's there." She launched my phone's browser and entered the street address. "It's a company. Voncabo Corporation."

"Voncabo? I've heard of them. They're a big time multinational company. Food and agriculture, I think. What do they do at the Woodland location?"

She punched the keys on my cell phone, waiting as a new webpage launched. She read silently for a few seconds. "Says here they produce genetically enhanced seeds. Tomatoes, beans, broccoli, and peppers."

"I have a bad feeling about this," I said to her. It took me ten minutes to get back on 113. I hit eighty miles an hour as we flew past Davis towards Woodland, following Rubia's directions.

"You're gonna need to go right at the next road, the first left after that." Five minutes later, Rubia announced we were less than a mile away.

The building sat all by itself off the country road surrounded by acres and acres of open space. About a quarter of a mile from the structure, I cut my headlights and slowed to about twenty miles an hour.

"Can you grab my camera bag?" I asked.

I pulled to the side of the road and took the camera bag from her. I removed my camera with the AstroScope telephoto lens I'd mounted on it prior to heading to Nimbus Dam. The lens was made for night shooting without a flash.

"Let's walk," I said.

We crouched as we walked towards the Voncabo building, using the occasional tree and shrub to shield us from view. About a hundred yards away, I spotted Seeger's car and snapped a photo of it with the building also in frame. I checked the camera's screen to make sure the license plate was readable.

"Call 9-1-1," I said. "Tell them what's going on."

While Rubia called, I tried to locate the two men. The building was two stories, with an L-shaped foundation, stucco siding, and a pitched roof punctuated with scores of tall cylindrical vents. I looked through the camera to aid my night vision, sweeping from one end of the building to the other. At the intersection of the two legs of the L, I saw movement, a man jogging back towards the car. I snapped a photo of him. I made another pass across the building with the camera and spotted a second man also heading towards the car. I took a shot of him, then put the camera strap around my neck and started to jog towards them. Rubia finished her call and joined me.

Less than a minute later, we were upon them. Both wore black ski masks and were about to enter Seeger's car when I drew my gun.

"Stop!" I called out.

Both of them snapped their attention in my direction. Rubia and I pointed guns at them.

"You're not getting away with this," I said.

"Fuck you." I recognized Seeger's nasally voice at once.

"You're a regular pain in the ass," Forrester added. "You're too late."

Rubia and I advanced upon them, drawing to within twenty feet or so.

"I scare you off the dam, and you come here instead. Just because you have three stacks of dynamite." I moved even closer, Rubia by my side. "You're like two kids who found a firecracker and just have to blow it up somewhere."

Forrester's face twitched a little. I'd surprised him by knowing how many bombs he had. "You didn't scare us off anything."

"Fine," I said, my gun pointed at his face ten feet away. "Now get back in there and take it all back. I want all three of the bundles disarmed and away from the building before the police get here in about three minutes." I looked over at Rubia to confirm the timing. She nodded.

"Fuck you," Forrester said. "How you going to make me do that?"

"I'll start by shooting you in the leg." I moved my aim from his head to his right leg. "And my colleague here will do the same with your boy Seth over there."

"Be my pleasure." She took aim at Seeger's leg.

"You're bluffing," he said. "Get in the car, Seth."

Forrester got into the passenger side of the car and shut the door. Seth slid behind the steering wheel, keeping his eye on Rubia's gun until he was inside. I fired and shot out his front tire. Seeger sped away, flat tire and all.

"What the hell?" Rubia said. "Why'd you let 'em slide?"

"We couldn't just shoot them. They were unarmed. We don't have time to talk. I need to get those bombs out of there."

"No, Ray. He said it was too late. You'll blow your ass up going in there."

"Forrester was working on something over in the middle of the building. You stay here, and I'll go check."

"No!" Rubia said grabbing my upper arm.

I started to shake my arm free, when I was knocked off my feet by a deafening blast. It felt as if someone had pushed me hard in the chest to topple me. I lifted my head and could see an eruption of flames at the building's core. My ears rang and my head pounded. Then, in quick succession came two more claps of thunder as loud as the first. I struggled to my feet, dazed and wobbling. Rubia still lay on the ground five feet from where she'd been standing. I rushed to her unmoving body.

I knelt beside her, fearing the worst. I put my hand to her cheek and then found a pulse point on the side of her neck.

"The hell you doing?" she asked, her eyes springing open.

"You scared me."

She raised herself up to her elbows and took a look at the scene in front of us. "Help a girl up?"

I put a hand under her arm and helped her to her feet, relieved she was okay.

We looked at the building. Both ends of it had been blown out. The explosion in the center had crumbled it, and flames shot a hundred feet into the air, spreading to engulf the rest of the building. The heat was so intense we had to draw back a hundred feet.

"Damn," Rubia said, though I could barely hear her over the ringing in my ears.

We beheld the conflagration and shook our heads, our efforts to avert disaster futile. I'd been unable to turn Riley Forrester or even the impressionable Seth Seeger. All of our reconnaissance yielded nothing more than a front row seat to horrible destruction. Nothing we could do now but wait for the police to arrive.

thirty-one

AT NOON THE NEXT DAY, I sat at a barstool and watched Rubia prepare the Say Hey for the early afternoon crowd. She refilled the refrigerators with beer and half a case of Chardonnay. While she did her stocking, I cut up celery stalks for the Bloody Marys and filled the garnish tray with Maraschino cherries, olives, and cocktail onions. We were both tired, having been detained at the Voncabo explosion site until three in the morning, first answering questions from Woodland police and fire, and then again when the FBI rolled in.

The FBI team originally dispatched to Nimbus Dam had hustled out to the scene. The lead fed, a guy named Burton, was not too happy to learn I'd been the anonymous tipster about the dam. I reminded them I'd provided them with Forrester's and Seeger's identities and had no idea they would change their target to Voncabo, but he was still pissed at me. I suppose he had a point. He was somewhat placated, though, when I showed him the photos I'd taken of the two terrorists moments before the blasts.

"Think the cops popped those two yet?" Rubia asked as she knelt in front of the refrigerator beneath the back bar.

"Unless they went on the run, I'm sure they have."

"Glad you took those pictures. Those should nail their asses. Those and our statements."

I shook my head. "It's going to be a long ordeal, you watch. They'll bring us into court to testify. I'll look forward to it. Looking both of them in the eyes."

"Oh, hey," she said, getting to her feet. "I heard from my LA guy."

"Your gang network friend?"

"Gang network, yeah, that's what it's called. Try colleague."

"Whatever. What did he say?"

"He's heard of both your guys, Wu Wing and Bo Chen."

"Yeah?"

"Wu's a lifer with the Golden Dragons down south. Been with them ever since he was twelve, thirteen years old. Started off selling weed and crystal on the street corners. Like they all do. He's been kind of middle management the last ten years or so. Not smart enough to go any higher."

"Why did he come up to Sacramento?"

"We figure Thomas Chan had some sort of connection in the Dragons or knew somebody who knew somebody. Anyway, word got out Chan needed a bunch of cash for his business."

"And the Dragons were more than happy to loan shark him a half-million dollars."

"Yeah."

"Wu saw it as his big chance. To be *jefe* up here. He asked to drive the cash up from LA and then see what other shit he could drum up. The banger he brought with him, Bo, is a lamester. The southern guys were more than happy to have him come up here, too."

I sipped my coffee and thought. It made sense. And Chan was stupid or naive enough to think he could borrow that much money and earn ten percent interest a week right off the bat.

"Did he have anything else to say about the gang or the two knuckleheads they sent up here?"

"Not so much." Rubia picked up the empty box she'd used to cart in the beer bottles and started for the trash in the back. "Oh, yeah." She turned around at the end of the bar. "Said the two fingers they cut off—the ring and index finger—was for sure Dragon shit. They think it's real funny, the 'fuck you' gesture and all."

"Yeah, real ha ha stuff."

"But he said it was weird the day after they cut off his fingers they killed him. Usually they cut off the two fingers to start then wait a week or two and cut off another finger. Makes people find the money someway, somehow. Like I said yesterday, killing someone right away means they wouldn't get paid."

"So Wu was impatient...and stupid," I said.

"Looks like."

"I still think they might have killed Chan to send a message to Benzer."

"Maybe."

She went out back with the empty box. I thought more about the Chan murder scene. Knifed on his bed. The bandage covering the two missing fingers from the day before now removed. The SCS scrawled in blood on the bedroom wall. My cell phone rang, interrupting my thoughts.

"This is Ray."

"What the hell have you gotten yourself into?" It was Trujillo getting back to me at last.

"You heard about Woodland, I'm guessing."

"First you're dealing with Chinese gangsters and now eco-terrorists?"

"All in a day's work."

"Seriously, what's going on?"

"It's kind of a long story. It's your Granderson referral."

"Granderson? Really? I thought that was a stolen term paper or something some grad student was worried about."

"Sort of. But it got a lot more complicated very fast." I drained the last of my coffee and set the mug down. "Nice of you to call me back finally."

"I've been busy," Trujillo said, the normal crankiness in his voice returning. "It's your damn fault. Those two thugs, the Chinese guys, ever since I collared them after you called, I've been in teleconferences and meetings trying to sort out who gets to charge them first, us or LAPD."

"Wait a minute. You have them under arrest?"

"Of course, we rolled on it the minute after you called. I thought you knew."

I exhaled into the phone, part relief, part irritation. I knew it would've taken the gangsters some time to identify and track me down, so my immediate safety hadn't been a big concern. But it would have been nice to know they'd been arrested. Even more critical was Benzer's need to know. They knew where he lived and worked. He'd gone into hiding once he left the hospital, which turned out to be an unnecessary precaution.

"How the hell would I know that?" I asked. "Benzer's gone underground fearing those goons were going to kill him."

"I know. I've been trying to find him ever since you called."

"You never talked to him?"

"By the time we got to the emergency room, he was gone."

"Gone?"

"Yeah, the ER receptionist said he got antsy and left before anyone looked at him. She said he seemed nervous."

Made sense. His injuries probably weren't life threatening and after what he'd been through, Benzer probably didn't want to sit anywhere he might be found by the gangsters.

"What about Wu and Bo? Did they cop to the Thomas Chan murder?"

"No. They won't admit to it, but we're trying to build a case. They said they didn't touch Benzer either."

"How can you hold them, then?"

"That's why I'm calling. I need you to come to the station and give testimony about what you saw them do to Benzer. For now, we have one of the neighbors who testified they saw the kid shooting the shotgun at a moving car, which I assume was yours. We also have two felons in possession of firearms and drugs."

"So they're going to be locked up for a while then?"

"Oh, yeah, they won't be offered bail. LAPD has outstanding warrants out on both of them. Manslaughter and aggravated assault. One way or another they'll be in jail for a long time."

We ended the call as Rubia returned to the bar. She looked around the interior of the Say Hey, nodded to confirm the place was ready for customers, and went to the front door to unlock it.

"What did you say was the name of the liquor store in Oroville? The one Benzer's parents owned."

"I didn't. Don't think my guy told me. But hell, professor, it's Oroville. How many ghetto marts you think there are?"

She was right. Oroville had a population of, at most, fifteen thousand. And the parents lived in an apartment above the store, making the search even easier. It was something of a long shot, but I didn't know enough about Adam Benzer to know where he might turn if he needed to disappear for a while. His parents might be one option.

An hour later, I rolled down Oroville's Olive Highway to the first liquor store that popped up when I entered "Oroville liquor stores" into the web browser on my cell phone. The store was in a strip mall, next to a gas station, across the street from Oroville Hospital. I pondered for a few seconds if being close to a hospital would be good or bad for a liquor store's business. Unable to come up with an answer, I nevertheless crossed Town & Country off the list because it lacked a second story, a requirement for an upstairs apartment. Glad to see my lack of sleep wasn't diminishing my reasoning skills.

I started to go to the second liquor store on the list—AJ's Food and Liquor—when I decided to review the entire list first. At the bottom of the seven stores listed, I found a Benzer's Liquors. My lightning powers of perception continued to dazzle me.

I parked in front of the store in downtown Oroville. The adjective "quaint" would best describe the four-square block downtown, whose streets were lined with bushy trees and pickup trucks. I smiled at a woman pushing a baby stroller as I walked by her and entered the store.

"Afternoon, there," a man's voice greeted me as soon as I entered.

I smiled and approached the counter, where he sat on a stool behind a cash register. The counter was cluttered with a plastic tub filled with mini bottles of vodka and four separate racks filled with plastic lighters, lotto scratchers, hangover pills, and Copenhagen. Behind the counter, to the side of a wall filled with liquor bottles, was an open doorway I guessed led to an office.

"Mr. Benzer?" I asked.

"You're not selling anything are you?"

"No, no, nothing like that."

"Because if you are I'd have to ask you to leave. You saw the sign on the door. No solicitors."

"No, not selling. Let me get right to the point. I'm looking for your son, Adam."

"Why?" He looked about sixty, bald and slender, though not in a fit way, his skin a bit on the pale side, and I noticed his index and middle fingered were browned from cigarette smoke.

"Is he here?"

"No." He said it so fast, his face turning to stone, I knew he was lying.

"I'm a friend. Or at least someone who's on his side, I guess is a better way to put it. You saw his face was a bit roughed up. I'm not sure if he told you about it, but I was there when…when it happened. I helped him. I took him to the hospital."

"Sorry, don't know what you're talking about. I haven't seen my son in months." He crossed his arms over his chest. A father hearing a report his son had been beaten would at least ask about his son's health. This man showed no concern at all.

"Have you heard from him?"

"No." The protective dad was not going to say word one about his son. I understood.

"If you do happen to see him, please give him my card." I reached into my breast pocket, pulled out a card, and handed it to him. He didn't reach for it, his arms still crossed, so I set the card on the counter. "Tell him the Chinese guys are in jail and will be there for a long time. Tell him he's safe."

"Like I said, I haven't seen him in months."

"It's okay, Dad," Adam Benzer said, stepping through the office doorway. He had a bandage next to his right eye and over the bridge of his nose.

I nodded at him. "You okay?"

"Yeah. I went to my doctor up here. He gave me a few stitches, and they had to reset my nose," he said, pointing at his face. "I've got a bruised kidney, but otherwise I'm okay."

I nodded. "They're both in jail. Police in at least two jurisdictions have charges against them. They won't be out anytime soon. Years, most likely."

"There'll be others. They'll want their money."

"I don't know about that, but for now I think you're safe."

He looked around the tiny liquor store. From the size of the store, I could tell the upstairs apartment had to be tiny, maybe the size of a cheap hotel room. Being cooped up there with your mom and dad couldn't be a load of fun.

"You're sure they're in jail?" he asked.

"Just talked to the police two hours ago. I wanted to let you know. It's up to you what you want to do."

thirty-two

ON THE DRIVE BACK FROM Oroville, I stopped at a Taco Bell and a Valero for a late lunch and to fill up my car. I was exhausted when I arrived home, so I allowed myself a thirty-minute nap. When I awoke three hours later, it was dark outside and I was hungry again. I went to Raley's Supermarket on Freeport and bought some eggs, cheese, and bacon so I could make myself an omelet.

Rather than drive straight home after completing my shopping, I decided to go by Benzer's apartment. The night was turning cold, a steady wind buffeting my car. A rainstorm was in the forecast for the next day, but it felt like the storm might come sooner. I cranked up the heater.

I couldn't view his unit from the street, so I got out of the car and entered the courtyard where I could see lights on in Benzer's apartment for the first time since I'd been checking it the last couple of days. I thought about going up to talk to him but figured I'd give him some distance for the time being. I drove around back to the complex's parking lot and saw Benzer's car parked in the spot designated for his apartment.

I called Trujillo and left him a message telling him Benzer was back in town and could be reached at home. Back at my house, I didn't feel like cooking up an omelet after all. I felt restless and couldn't figure out why. The missing twenty million still bugged me, but there was more. It was now ten o'clock. I picked up a chicken sandwich and fries at Dad's Restaurant and took it with me to the Say Hey.

Two guys and a woman were sitting at a table watching the Kings game on the corner television. The only other customer, a middle-aged guy, was leaving as I entered. Rubia read a paperback as she leaned against the bar.

"Busy night," I said, settling on a barstool. "I thought you packed them in when the Kings played."

She didn't look up from her book. "You seen their record? They've won twelve games."

"If you're not too busy there, would you mind pouring me a Panic IPA?"

"Hold on." She continued to read.

I frowned at her. "What, are you at the part of the book where the wolf is about to blow down the straw house?"

"Ha, ha. It just happens to be…oh, fuck you. What'd you want?" She set down the book and moved towards the row of draft beer taps behind her.

"Panic IPA."

She gave me a mock dirty look when she set the beer in front of me. I smiled at her while I pulled out the chicken sandwich and french fries.

"You got some nerve bringing outside food into my bar."

"You don't serve food. Unless you count those frozen microwave burritos."

She reached over and took half my sandwich. "Thank you."

"You're welcome."

We ate our late dinner in silence for several minutes. Rubia resumed reading while polishing off her half of the sandwich and most of the fries. I watched the game on the TV at the end of the bar. For once the Kings were making it close, trailing by one point with eight seconds to go. They inbounded the ball and passed it to their best shooter, who missed a fifteen-foot jumper. The Kings's center grabbed the rebound but missed the put back shot and the Kings lost.

"Anything on Forrester and his *compinche*?" Rubia asked.

"Don't you read the newspaper or watch TV? It's all over the news. They've both been arrested. With the flat tire they didn't make it two miles before the cops found them."

"Still say you should've lit up his leg."

"They caught them. That's the main thing."

"If you don't mind my asking, why the hell you here at ten o'clock at night? Isn't it past bed time?"

"I'm feeling a little restless."

"Restless."

"I don't know. I found Benzer. He was up at his parents' place in Oroville."

"Was he cool the guys beat him up are in jail?"

"Seems so. He's back at his apartment."

"You got it all done, Ray. Got the goons who killed Chan. Got the eco-terrorists. Got Adam Benzer settled into his apartment."

I frowned at her. "I've got twenty million dollars still missing. And a blown up seed manufacturing plant."

"Never said you're perfect." She picked up my empty glass, re-filled it, and set it back onto the bar.

"I don't know. There are so many moving parts on this one, and they have to be connected. I'm just missing how."

"Maybe your head's gettin' in the way.

"Maybe."

I sat and drank in silence, rolling things over in my mind for a good ten minutes when my cell phone rang in my pocket. I pulled it out and checked caller ID. Sacramento Police Department.

"When did Benzer return home?" Nick Trujillo asked when I answered, skipping the formalities.

"Why?"

"Answer the question?"

"I don't know. I saw he was in his apartment when I left you the message. So it was sometime before that. I met with him in Oroville mid-afternoon so sometime between then and when I called you."

"Okay," he said, pausing to write or think it over.

"Are you going to tell me what's going on?"

Rubia looked at me with curiosity. I shrugged at her and mouthed Trujillo's name.

"Yeah, be glad to. Benzer's dead. Somebody shot him in his apartment. After you called, I go over to talk to him, to get a statement about his dealings with the Golden Dragons. He doesn't answer his door. I can hear music inside, and there's a gap in his curtains where I can see a lot of blood on his carpet. I call for backup before I bust in. Boom. The guy's dead with three gunshot wounds in his chest."

I was stunned. Benzer dead. And I was the one who told him eve-rything was clear, and it was safe to return to Sacramento. I shoved the glass of beer to the side, my head feeling light all of a sudden. I took a deep breath, but it didn't help.

"Do you know who did it?" I managed to ask.

"No, we don't have squat. Looks like he let the killer in, and the guy shot him. No signs of a break in or a struggle."

I could feel the blood pounding in my head as I tried to put this news into perspective with everything else. "Wu and Bo. Are they still in jail?" I grasped at the notion the two might have been granted an ill-advised bail release.

"Yeah, locked up tight. But guess what? They didn't kill Thomas Chan."

"Why do you say that? They cut off his fingers and—"

"They may have cut off his fingers, but they didn't kill him. We have cell phone records that put both of them in eastern Eldorado County at the time Chan was killed in Sacramento. We have a confirmed sighting at a restaurant about forty miles from Chan's place. Two eyewitnesses saw both of our guys eating at the Silver Fox Diner at the time the coroner said Chan died. They're clean on the murder at least. With your testimony, we still have enough to put them away on the Benzer assault. My guess is we'll end up turning them over to LAPD."

We ended the call. Trujillo said he wanted to talk more the next day, but I didn't know what else I could tell him. I dropped my face into my hands and stared at the top of the bar.

"What?" Rubia asked.

I looked at her, my mind turning everything over and over. Benzer was dead. Impossible.

"I've been played," I said.

thirty-three

I WAITED IN THE SMUD lobby Monday morning, looking at their large multimedia message board featuring closed captioned videos on energy-efficient products, a weather report, digital clock, and a map showing power outages in their service territory. At the moment, dozens of red dots were indicating customers who were without power. Outside, the predicted storm had hit with a bang, the rain coming down in buckets starting in the middle of the night and with no end in sight. The streets in my neighborhood had started to flood, so the five-mile drive to SMUD took forty-five minutes. The wind whistled through the twin glass doors at the front of the building, and the security guard left his security desk to lock one of the doors to prevent it from blowing open. The second door continued to swing open a foot or two when a particularly strong gust of wind hit. The guard and I exchanged shrugs. Not much he could do short of locking down the building.

Roger Talbert emerged from an elevator on the other side of the security desk and entered the lobby through a short swinging gate.

"I figured it would be easier coming down here to meet you than having you clear security all over gain." Roger and I shook hands. "Helluva storm," he said, looking through the front glass windows.

"Thanks for meeting with me on such short notice." I had called him about an hour before. "I know how busy you are. I wanted to follow up on our conversation the other day about Chan International."

168

"I can't believe Benzer was murdered. I saw it on the morning news. It's horrible. Do the police know who did it? It's got to be whoever killed Thomas Chan."

"Yeah, that'd be my guess. They were wrapped up with some loan sharks."

"Not good. So, I'm guessing that's where the payoff money came from?"

I nodded. "Yep."

"So, are the loan sharks the killers?"

"Nope," I said, shaking my head.

He looked surprised. "How do you know that?"

"It's a long story. And a complicated one. That's kind of why I'm here, Roger. I'm trying to figure it out." A huge gust of wind hurtled against the glass, lurching open the door and littering the entryway with rain and loose leaves.

"Are you working with the police or something?"

"Not really. I'm working a different angle, I guess you could say." I didn't want to get into the whole backstory, and I doubted he would have been interested anyway.

"I don't know if I can provide much help. Our dealings with Chan and the printer in China have been pretty straightforward once we got past the bribe thing."

"Benzer came here a couple of days ago," I said. "What did he want?"

Roger gave me a blank look. "Are you sure? He didn't come to see me. I haven't seen him in weeks."

He surprised me, but only a little. "He told me he came to see you, but he could have been lying. Would he have come to see somebody else?"

Roger thought for a moment, staring vacantly ahead. I could tell he was still shaken up by Chan and Benzer. Then a switch went off in his head, and his eyes regained their focus. "Leo Farrell. He's the head of our renewable energy program. I ran into him the other day, and he asked me about Benzer and about Chan International. He said Benzer had called him out of the blue and pitched him on something. Benzer used me as a reference to set up the meeting. Leo said he looked at our contract records to validate that Benzer's firm was doing business with us. Once he confirmed it, he set the meeting. I think they met a couple of days ago."

"What did Benzer pitch him?"

"I don't know," Roger said with a shrug. "Leo just said it was a strange meeting. Said Benzer was squirrelly and nervous."

"Do you think I could talk to this Leo?"

"Sure, but probably not today. I heard he went out to our PV farm to make sure they were okay in the storm."

"PV farm?"

"Photovoltaic panels. We have a couple of acres of them out by Rancho Seco. I suppose you could go out there and try and catch up with him."

Driving thirty-five miles to Rancho Seco in the worst storm of the winter did not rank high on my list of desired activities. Southbound traffic on Highway 99 crawled along, the road a veritable river. I counted six separate cars that slid off to the side of the road, driving too fast for conditions and colliding with the cement sidewall. It took well over an hour to reach the Arno Road exit in the southernmost part of Sacramento County, a rural, unincorporated area marked by its flat landscape and cattle farms. I feared the fifteen miles of country roads leading to Rancho Seco might be even more problematic than 99 had been. Creeks tended to overflow and spill onto roads in this part of the county. If I encountered a flooded road, I would have to either turn around or risk getting stranded.

After a few miles, the rain let up, though the wind, if anything, intensified. At one point, a row of four wooden power poles had toppled, their power lines draped over a stretch of barbed wire fencing. In the distance, I could see Rancho Seco, even in the rain not a difficult feat considering the twin cooling towers were more than four hundred feet tall.

I arrived at the front gate to the shuttered nuclear power plant thirty minutes later. Rancho Seco had been built in the 1970s when nuclear power was being hailed as our energy future, producing electricity that supposedly would be too cheap to even meter. After the nuclear accident at Three Mile Island, Rancho Seco had its own set of problems, from technical to managerial, and was inactive more than it ran until the voters of Sacramento decided to shut it down for good in 1989. The area around the plant became a recreation area, with fishing, boating, hiking, and picnicking the favored activities around the lake created as the water supply to cool nuclear fuel rods. Somewhere along the line, a photovoltaic farm had been added to the vast acreage. A simple wooden sign pointed me in the direction of the PV site.

Outfitted in hiking boots, blue jeans, a blue rain slicker, and a San Francisco Giants baseball hat, I set off from my car through the open chain link gate and towards rows and rows of photovoltaic panels. Propelled by the surging wind, the few drops of rain continuing to fall stung my face as I searched for Leo Farrell.

Each row contained about twenty of the ten-foot-wide panels standing about twelve feet high. Gravel had been laid down between the rows, but the rain had been so heavy, mud oozed up from underneath, and I gave up trying to keep my boots clean. I passed by seven or eight rows, pausing at each one to see if anyone was inspecting the panels. A couple of rows later, I spotted a white pickup truck at the other end. I walked between the two sets of panels and reached the truck, finding it empty. A few feet away, a man dressed head-to-toe in yellow rain gear worked on the underside of a panel. A large red tool kit sat on the gravel beside him.

"Hey," I said from a few feet away. He didn't hear me, the wind too loud as it whistled through the gaps in the panels. "Leo Farrell," I said, louder this time, moving closer.

He looked up, saw me, and then continued to work. A minute later, he stood, tossed the wrench into the tool kit, and turned to me. "Damn trackers are always coming loose. The wind does it. Not that it matters much today. It's not a good day to be generating sun power. But I came all the way out here. May as well make myself useful."

I introduced myself, and he confirmed he was indeed Leo Farrell. He was about forty, a big guy, at least six-three and more than two hundred pounds, with a bushy brown mustache.

"What can I do for you?" he asked.

I told him I was an investigator looking into recent business dealings involving Chan International. He took the information at face value, expressing no curiosity about what exactly I was investigating. If he knew anything about the Chan and Benzer killings he said nothing about it. We had to speak just beneath a shout to make ourselves heard as the wind slapped our clothes and pounded the photovoltaic panels.

He pointed at his ear and then at the truck. "Mind if we get in?"

We walked to his pickup truck, Farrell toting his tool kit. He slung the kit into the large box in back.

"I understand you met with Adam Benzer a couple of days ago," I said once we'd settled into the truck.

"Yeah, I met with him." He blew into his cupped hands to warm them.

"May I ask what you two talked about?"

"Sure." He slid back the hood of the slicker to reveal a head of light brown hair as thick as his mustache. "He called me. Said he had a deal for me. I get that all the time. You know, companies trying to sell me this technology or that."

"So he was trying to pitch you on a product."

"Yep. I don't meet with people who call me out of the blue, but he said he knew Roger Talbert. Roger's a good guy. Runs our corporate communications department."

"I know Roger. He was a student of mine back at Sac State."

"You're a professor?"

"Was. Retired now."

"Anyway, he checked out. I saw Roger did have a printing contract with him. And their company website looked legit, so I called him back and said I could spare a half hour to talk with him."

"So, what was he trying to sell you?"

"Fuel cells." Farrell rubbed a hand through his thick mane. "I mean it was more than just fuel cells. It was cutting-edge technology. I'd never even heard of anything as advanced as he described."

"Wait a second. He was selling you a cutting-edge fuel cell or the rights to the technology, or what exactly?"

"He said his client would turn over to me all of their research data, including their sequencing for the microbial genomes and a prototype for the fuel cells themselves. Plus, SMUD would be given the rights to patent everything. The way he described it, the fuel cells were more scaleable than anything else out on the market right now. They could be used for powering anything from a car to a small city."

Monarch. "Did he have anything to show you?"

"No. And I could tell he knew little about the science or technology. He was a business guy, not a scientist or engineer. That made me a little leery. I told him I'd need to see a formal proposal, with specs, drawings, the whole nine yards."

"What did he say to that?"

"He said he could get all the information to us next week as long as we were willing to buy. That made me laugh. He obviously didn't know much about SMUD. We can't move that fast. We're a public agency. Everything we do needs to be competitively bid. Something on the order of what he was describing would take months, if not a year or more, to set up. We had to create an RFP with specifications and selection criteria and then set up a review committee."

"But if it was one-of-a-kind technology, couldn't you sole source it?"

"Not really. I told him if he brought me the specs then we could write the request for proposals in a way to make it easier for him to win the proposal."

"What do you mean?"

"It was unlikely anyone had technology like what he was talking about. I go to conferences all the time and stay current with what's out there. I've never heard anything like what he had. So I told him we could write the specs to fit his technology."

"Was he interested?"

"He got excited. But then I told him even it would take a few months. He said he needed to sell it by next week or the week after at the latest. He got a little ticked off at me when I laughed. I said I couldn't buy much more than a box of pencils in a week or two. Not with SMUD's bureaucracy and rules."

"If you don't mind telling me, how much was he asking for the technology and everything?"

"That's where he got squirrelly." Farrell looked at me and shook his head.

Squirrelly. That's what he had told Roger.

"He started off asking five million dollars. When I kept telling him how long it would take SMUD to do a deal like that, he must have thought I was negotiating because he kept dropping the price. By the time he walked out, the deal on the table was a half-million dollars. That's what made me doubt what he had. If he had what he described, it would've been worth hundreds of millions of dollars, maybe more. For him to try selling it for a half-million didn't make sense."

thirty-four

THE WIND AND RAIN BATTERED Sacramento well into the afternoon. KFBK radio warned of flood conditions in several parts of town and power outages caused by falling trees and toppled power lines. I parked my car in the former cannery's parking lot and sat for a moment as the rain hammered my car. I picked up my gym bag and jogged towards the door of Alhambra Athletic Club as the rain soaked my clothes.

It had been weeks since Rubia and I had played a game of HORSE, a basketball shooting tradition we'd been doing for at least five years. We tried to play once a week, but our work schedules and other obligations had gotten in the way.

Today, our usual spot, an outdoor court in Reichmuth Park, was out of the question in the storm, so she insisted I meet her at her hoity-toity gym east of downtown. I agreed after she said she would pay the fifteen-dollar guest fee.

"I'm not up for this right now," I said. We had just walked onto the half-court basketball surface that also served as space for aerobics, yoga, and tae kwon do classes.

"Man up," Rubia said.

As usual, we shot around for ten or fifteen minutes before starting our game of HORSE, the object of which was to make a shot your opponent cannot. If you made it and he missed, then he got a letter in the word horse. Once the entire word was spelled out, because the person had missed more shots than his opponent, then he lost the game. I hadn't beaten Rubia in four years, meaning she'd received four years of breakfasts on me.

My mind wasn't on the game when I lined up the opening shot, a fifteen-foot jumper from the baseline. Benzer had knowledge of Monarch. Not only that, he believed he had enough access to it to get ahold of it and sell it to SMUD. It's unlikely he'd have approached Leo Farrell with his proposition if he'd been the extortionist, twenty million dollars in hand. Unless he was double dipping, having pocketed the twenty million and now adding on by selling a copy of Monarch to SMUD. In any case, Chan had to be the link to the project, either from his girlfriend Candace, Wiggin, or Jack Cassidy. Chan and Benzer were linked, both with knowledge about Monarch.

My shot from the baseline drew nothing but air, falling a good two feet short of the basket.

"That's sad, Ray. At least try to give me a game."

Rubia prepared for her favorite opening shot, a cross over dribble and a reverse layup. I thought back about the drop night. Corti Brothers, where I found the note directing me to Effie Yeaw Nature Center. There, another note directed me to Sand Cove. I'd left the keys underneath the van and walked to the Virgin Sturgeon. The bartender got a call telling me it was okay to go back to my car.

Rubia, as usual, made her shot. For an ex-gangbanger with no formal coaching, she was a natural athlete with amazing basketball skills. Had her life traveled a different path, she might have been a Division-I college athlete, maybe even a WNBA player.

She sent me a crisp chest pass after rebounding her own shot. I had to repeat her shot and make it to avoid getting an H, something for which I held low expectations.

I received two calls that night, one from Wiggin and one from Candace. They wanted to know how things were going and if I was safe. At the time, I'd not thought much of it. Now I wondered if they'd been wondering whether I was on track to make the drop off on time at Sand Cove, where one or more of them would take the money.

I missed my attempt to replicate Rubia's shot.

Something about my last conversation with Trujillo came to mind. What did he say? Think. Cell phone records had put Wu and Bo in Eldorado County. Cell companies could tell where you made your phone calls based on which cell phone tower picked up your signal and directed the call.

"Hey," I said. "You still have the friend who works at AT&T?"

Rubia nodded. I gave her the names and dates for the cell records I wanted checked, and she promised to do it, "as soon as I'm done kicking your ass in HORSE."

I wanted the information and was tempted to throw the game, but my competitiveness kicked in. Twenty minutes later, both of us were sitting on HORS.

"I'm calling swish," she said standing at the three-point arc. Swish meant she would make the shot hitting nothing on the basket but the net. As called, she hit the shot, barely rustling the net, putting the pressure on me to make the same perfect shot.

I took the ball and set for the shot.

"Hey," she said. "You got to be behind the line."

I took two steps back, dribbled three times and took the jumper. The ball rattled around the rim and dropped through. I'd made the shot, but lost the game.

"Swish," I said. "You really want to win that way?"

"Heh, heh. Pancake Circus tomorrow at seven. I'm going to be big-time hungry."

"What's new?"

We headed to our respective locker rooms to shower and change back into our street clothes. When I exited the men's locker room, Rubia was sitting at a table in the lobby talking on her cell phone. I sat down next to her, and she held up a finger before ending the call a few seconds later.

"No records for Candace Symington or Jack Cassidy. They must have different cell providers. I only have a contact at AT&T. But I did find what you were looking for on Wiggin."

"Are you going to tell me or continue to gloat over your basketball victory?"

"Touchy, touchy." She gave me a too-cute smile. "Okay, here's what's up. Wiggin's in Germany on the dates you mentioned. Made lotsa calls and got dinged for international charges."

"What about the other night, when I was making the drop?"

"You gonna let me finish?"

I rolled my eyes and slumped down in my seat.

"At six forty-seven the night he called your cell. The call went less than a minute and routed through cell tower 8114 on Garden Highway, the thirty-three hundred block to be exact."

"Did he make any other calls around that time?"

"No."

I pulled up the map feature on my cell phone and punched in the Garden Highway address. As I suspected, the cell tower was about a half-mile from Sand Cove Park Beach. I jumped up to leave, almost forgetting the gym bag I'd set at my feet.

"You're welcome, Ray."

I turned and looked back over my shoulder. "Hey, I'm buying you breakfast tomorrow. Isn't that thanks enough?"

She flipped me off as I turned and headed out of the club.

Banned or not, nothing was going to keep me from venturing on-to the Granderson University campus. I parked in the visitor lot and hustled to Sieboldt. Wiggin sat alone at his desk working his laptop. It was a quarter to five in the afternoon.

"Making another run at the Minesweeper record?" I asked, sitting down uninvited in one of the chairs across from him.

"Oh, hey," he said. "Check it out, dude." He turned his laptop around so I could see the screen. The header on the webpage read "Minesweeper Game World Rankings." Beneath this was a numbered list of names, the flag of the person's country of origin, a time and a date. Number one on the list: Kenneth Wiggin, USA, 35.58. According to the date listed, he had set the record earlier in the day.

"Congratulations. You must be proud."

"Bet your ass. I've been shooting for the record for years. I'm pumped."

"Better celebrate."

He turned the laptop back around and looked at the screen, beaming at what he saw.

"You called me the other night," I said.

He looked at me, puzzled. "Oh, yeah, you mean when you were delivering the money."

I nodded.

"You were great, man. Thank you again for all you did. I would've been too nervous to drive all over town like they had you do. It was cool, the way you handled things."

"Getting back to your call, turns out it came from an area about a half-mile from Sand Cove Beach, where I dropped off the money."

He didn't react one way or the other to my statement.

"Kind of a coincidence, don't you think?"

"I guess it is. I was at my sister's, housesitting while she and her husband and kids were in Washington D.C. on vacation. I was looking after their Golden Retriever."

"And your sister lives over by the river?"

"On Delta Queen Avenue. Wouldn't get me to live that close to the river. It would scare the shit out of me on days like today. I checked the news website and the Sacramento River is close to over-flowing. My sister's putting out sandbags as we speak. She even—"

I raised my palm to stop him. "So, wait, you say you were hous-esitting when I was driving around with all the money and your project's future was on the line?"

"Yeah, so?"

"Again, kind of a coincidence you were near where I dropped off the money."

He finally seemed to see where I was going. "What? You think I ransomed my own project? Why the hell would I want to do that?"

"Twenty million bucks."

He laughed. "I should be insulted. But I think it's kind of funny. Kenneth Wiggin, Master Criminal." He posed like he was holding a machine gun and moved it from one side of the room to the other.

"You were so nonchalant about the whole thing. You didn't seem worried at all the project had gone missing. I thought that was strange."

"You're serious." His smile evaporated. "You think I took my own project?"

"What I'm still not sure about is why you looped in Chan and Benzer. Was the whole thing their idea? Did they approach you, and you thought 'Cool, dudes, let's get us some righteous bones'?"

"I don't like what you're saying," Wiggin said, all traces of the surfer dude gone from his voice and demeanor.

"It makes perfect sense. I feel like an idiot for not thinking of it sooner. I'm not sure how you were able to erase all traces of the project from Jack's and Candace's computers. Maybe they're in on it, too. Stealing the server had to involve somebody on campus. Again, either Jack or Candace. Or maybe Benzer and Chan. Which of them was it? Or were all of you in on it?"

He looked away, his jaw flexing, arms held tight across his chest.

"Who else was in on it?"

He now stared at me with steel in his eyes. I thought he might throw the laptop at me, and I prepared to duck.

"Get the fuck out of here!" he yelled. "Right now! And if I hear you tell your theory to anyone else, I will sue your ass so fast it will make your head spin. Did you hear me?"

He didn't throw the laptop, but he did throw a box of tissues, hitting me square in the chest. I'd pushed him to his limit, and he'd not admitted a thing. I picked up the box from the floor, stood up, and slammed it onto his desk. I backed towards the door, pausing as I reached it.

"I'm not done yet," I said. "Not by a long shot." I left his office, Sieboldt Hall, and Granderson University with the storm still raging in the February night.

thirty-five

RETURNING HOME AFTER MY ENCOUNTER on the Granderson campus, I couldn't sit down as I bustled about the house, fuming at myself, at Wiggin, at the whole sordid mess surrounding Monarch. Some of what happened began to take shape. It was an inside job all the way. Kenneth Wiggin had to be involved. Maybe even Candace Symington and Jack Cassidy. Somewhere, somehow, Thomas Chan and Adam Benzer came into the mix. Then there was Riley Forrester and the SCS, and Seth Seeger and S-SOP. It was an alphabet soup of names and acronyms. And everybody seemed to have been lying.

I needed a play to make all the parts come together, so I could see it more clearly. I spent a good two hours pacing from room to room, trying to recall the details of every interaction I'd had with everyone involved with the Monarch mess. I stopped in my tracks between the kitchen and the living room. From my office, I retrieved my laptop and toted it to the dining room and set it on the table. Five minutes later, I found a website called Marinetitle.com and bought a thirty-day membership for thirty bucks. I tried several different search criteria before scoring a hit. I wrote down the information on a notepad and folded down the laptop screen.

The view from my kitchen window confirmed what my ears had told me before—the wind and rain had stopped for now. It was after ten o'clock, but I knew I couldn't sleep, so I put on a thick jacket, grabbed a Mag light and camera bag, and headed for my car parked in the driveway.

My first stop was Sand Cove, where I was disappointed to find the gate to the drive leading to the parking lot locked. I parked in the narrow space between Garden Highway and the gate. The road to the parking lot sloped downhill. I walked carefully down the road, the flashlight guiding me. At the end of the road it became clear why the gate had been closed—the parking lot was flooded in several inches of water. I didn't care as I slogged along, arriving at the midpoint of the cement patch, my running shoes saturated as I stood in water above my ankles. In my previous visit I hadn't given much significance to how close I was to the river. In front of where I stood, a dirt path curved down to a narrow beach.

When I sat at the bar at the Virgin Sturgeon that night, I kept picturing a van or truck pulling into this parking lot, the occupants hoisting the bags from the van into their vehicle. The possibility they might have used a boat didn't enter my mind. Access to the parking lot from the water was ideal for transferring the money from the van onto a boat. I thought about walking down the path towards the river, then thought better of it. Any footprints or other signs of activity down at the beach would have been washed away by the storm.

I returned to my car and started it up. The next destination was about a half-mile away. Riverview Marina had a covered parking structure cast in a dull blue-gray light. At this time of night no one else was present. I walked from the structure down the gangway to see four covered docking areas and two uncovered ones. They were all dimly lit with pole-top mounted florescent lights. Naively, I thought I could just walk down to the docking areas and inspect the names and vessel numbers of each boat until I found the one I was looking for.

"Damn!" I said when I reached the metal door preventing entry into the docks.

I went back to my car and retrieved my camera, the AstroScope lens still attached. I moved carefully on the sodden bank of the river paralleling the marina. None of the boats at the uncovered docks looked big enough. The boat I was looking for was thirty-four feet long.

I moved up the bank, the camera over my shoulder, spraying the flashlight from boat to boat as they bobbed in the dark water. My inspection of the first two covered docks took a few minutes. Steadying my progress with my uphill hand on the sloping bank, I reached a point where I could see most of the boats at the last two docks. The flashlight revealed at least five boats that could be thirty-four feet. When I turned off the light and raised the camera to examine the boats, I slipped and slid down the bank, my feet hitting the cold water. I reached up with my left hand and grabbed a handful of thick grass. Some of the grass pulled out from the saturated soil, but enough of it held to stop me going into the water beyond my knees.

I cursed and crawled partway up the bank until the footing felt firm enough to use the camera. I was looking for a boat named *Cardinal Rules*. I eliminated all but two of the boats based on their names. The bows of the two remaining boats faced me so I couldn't see any names painted on their sides or back. I cursed again. Why hadn't I brought a picture of what the boat looked like? That gave me an idea.

I dialed Rubia. She picked up on about the tenth ring.

"Hey, can you do me a favor?" I asked.

"Damn, Ray. What time is it? Woke me up."

"It's not even midnight. You shouldn't be asleep already. Not at your age."

"Whatcha want?"

"Can you find a photo of a boat and send it to me?"

"A photo of a boat? What, you forget what a boat looks like?"

"Not any boat, a particular boat. Write it down."

"Don't know why I put up with you."

"Because I'm so charming."

She sighed. "Hold on." I could hear her moving around her apartment. "Okay."

"Look up a Carver 404 Cockpit Motor Yacht built in 1999."

"Why don't you do it?"

"At the moment I'm standing on the bank of the Sacramento River freezing my ass off, holding a flashlight, a camera, and a cell phone. Adding a web search might be a bit challenging. Oh, and if you can find it send a shot of the boat looking at the front end."

"I'd ask why you're standing out there in the middle of the night, but I don't really care."

"Thank you."

She said she'd text me the photo as soon as she could. I waited for a few minutes, shivering. When my phone dinged announcing the message's arrival, I opened it. She'd come through, sending a front-on view of a Carver 404 that looked straight from a boat broker's website. I compared the photo to the boats at the dock. Not the same. Not even close.

Disappointed, I managed, after a few missteps, to make it back up the bank and to my car. I was wet and muddy from the fall. I cranked up the heater to stave off the chills and clear the windows fogging from my breath. The next stop was the Riverbank Marina a mile away. Riverbank was larger with a dozen different docking areas, most of which were covered. I repeated the same process as I had at Riverview with the same results, though I did manage to avoid falling into the river this time.

I questioned the wisdom of my search. My hope was the boat would be located as near as possible to Sand Cove, the simplest scenario for the extortionist to execute. When I thought about it more, however, I realized he could have kept the boat docked anywhere and still navigated to the drop site.

It was after one in the morning. I was wet, tired, cold, and cranky. I wanted a shower, a drink, and a warm bed. After a long, frustrating day, this needle in a haystack search seemed futile at best.

"You're an idiot, Ray," I said to myself.

At least Sacramento Marina was on the way home. The city-run facility was the area's largest, with more than four hundred slips. It wasn't located in the ritziest part of town but was at the end of Broadway that had given way to federal housing projects, petroleum processing facilities, and homeless encampments. A light rain started to fall, the front end of the new storm predicted to hit Sacramento before daybreak. I continued west on Broadway as it narrowed and ended with a sweeping left turn onto Marina View Drive, which led to an empty parking lot.

At the west end of the parking lot closest to the river sat the marina's office building, a handsome white structure stretching across the width of the six rows of parking spaces. There were enough light poles to ensure no one else was in the area, but to be sure, I took a lap around the lot before parking on the south side. The view from the parking lot did not hearten me. The five covered docks below ran away from me, blocking clear sightlines to the farthest boats. Across the way at Miller Park, I might be able to get a view of at least some of these, but not all. I zipped up my jacket and brought my camera and flashlight to find, as I had now come to expect, a security gate and razor wire preventing access to the docks.

The vantage point on the other side of the gate did reveal that most of the slips were empty. The remaining boats, even the parts I could glimpse at the farthest dock, were smaller than the one I was looking for.

The north side of the parking lot provided the same visual challenges as those on the south. I did notice a parking lot to my right offering a better view, but for now the only boats I could see were at the first of six docks. I walked towards the office building and observed the boats on this side of the marina were bigger, more on the order of what I was searching for. With my camera, I scanned the sterns of the dozens of boats, reading the names painted on them. At the western end of that first row I saw it: *Cardinal Rules.*

Now the question was how I would get aboard the damn boat.

thirty-six

THE DOUBLE SHOT OF KNOB Creek bourbon after a long hot shower helped me fall asleep about three in the morning. When I awoke at seven I felt rested and clear-headed. It would be a long day, so I made myself a big breakfast of eggs, bacon, a piece of toast, and an apple, washing it down with a glass of water and two cups of coffee.

The second storm front that had started when I was at the marina had come and gone, the street in front of my house glistening under a bright blue sky, a thin trickle of water easing down the gutter to the storm drains the last vestiges of the storm. I checked my cell and confirmed I'd received no new phone, e-mail, or text messages during my short sleep. Next, I punched in the phone number to my neighbors Ron and Carla Phillips.

I'd known Ron and Carla eighteen years now, ever since Pam, Sarah, and I had first moved into the neighborhood. They lived three doors down, both retired from their state jobs. Ron and I shared a passion for baseball and had countless conversations over the years about the merits of the designated hitter, the long ball versus little ball, pitch counts, instant replay for balls and strikes, and myriad other minutiae about the sport.

Ron greeted me enthusiastically. We exchanged small talk about the storm, the upcoming spring training season, and an update on a kitchen remodel they were about to undertake.

"I was calling to ask a favor," I said after we had exhausted the pleasantries.

"No, problem. What can I do for you?"

"I'll make it worth your trouble," I continued. "Box seats for you and Carla opening day, Giants and Dodgers, if I can borrow your boat for the morning. Unless you were planning to use it." He had a little twelve-foot aluminum fishing boat with an outboard motor on it.

"No, I wasn't going to go fishing today. Water's too stirred up from the rain. Hell yes, you can use it. And it's nice of you to offer, but you don't have to buy me tickets."

"I'm going to need to borrow your truck, too. I don't have a hitch on my car. And I'm getting you the tickets, so don't argue."

"Hell, for those opening day box seats against the Dodgers, you can borrow my boat and my truck. Want me to throw Carla in on the deal, too?"

I laughed. "No, the boat and truck are plenty."

Twenty minutes later, Ron was laughing when I told him I—a boating novice—was going out alone and didn't have anyone to help me launch it into the water. He offered to help me, but I didn't want to get him involved with what I was about to do. Instead, he walked me through the steps on how to accomplish a solo boat launch. Then I headed out for Miller Park.

The rain had dissuaded fishermen and other recreational boaters from going out on the river. I had the boat ramp all to myself. My skills towing trailers had never been a strong suit, so it took me nine or ten attempts to back the damn boat straight into the water. I hopped out of the truck and clipped one end of the nylon line to the bow of the boat and the other to an eye-bolt on the trailer, just as Ron had instructed. Returning to the truck, I backed up a few feet more until the boat was floating in the water, the rear wheels of the truck just touching the water's edge. Again, I got out of the truck, unclipped the line from the trailer, walked over to the adjacent pier, and tied the line to one of the several cleats running along the length of the pier.

I drove the truck back to the lot and parked it. Walking back to the boat, I boarded it and shoved off from the pier, gathering in the rope and starting the motor. For about five minutes, I practiced maneuvering the boat in the middle of the slow-moving river, gauging the throttle settings needed for docking speed and the sensitivity of the tiller. The river was a good two hundred feet wide, providing plenty of room for practice. Once I was satisfied I'd mastered the basic skills for my task, I navigated into the nearby inlet leading to the Sacramento

Marina, passed by the southern set of docks before drawing even with the marina office and parking lot. I eased up on the throttle a bit so I could get a view of the parking lot between the office and a stand of trees. From what I could tell, no one was parked in the lot and no lights shone through the office window. I cruised into the northern set of docks, where I spotted the *Cardinal Rules* on the first dock at the end nearest to me.

With the throttle set low, I puttered along at a couple of miles an hour. Three Canadian geese cruised by in the opposite direction, oblivious to my presence. The berths next to the *Cardinal Rules* were occupied, but I found a vacant one five spots away. I cut the engine and used a paddle to work my way close enough to the pier to grab one of the cleats. I tied the bowline to one cleat, got out of the boat, and tied the stern line to a second cleat.

Reaching into the boat, I pulled out a small plastic garbage bag where I'd placed my camera and cell phone to keep them dry. I stuck the cell phone in the pouch at the front of my UCLA Law hoodie and put the camera's strap around my neck.

My nerves kicked in as I contemplated for the first time whether somebody might be living on the *Cardinal Rules*. I dismissed the idea, for right or wrong, because no cars were parked in the nearby lot.

Toting the plastic bag, I moved down the dock to the *Cardinal Rules*. The boat's gunwale was too narrow to climb aboard from the pier. The stern looked more promising, where a wide foot ledge provided access to a cabin door. I tried the brass door handle and found it locked. When I reached into my rear pants pocket for the lock pick set, I cursed silently. I'd set the damn thing on the floor of Ron's boat because it was too uncomfortable to sit on.

I went back to Ron's boat to retrieve the pick set. Unable to reach it from the pier, I stepped on the middle bench seat and reached over to grab it. As I did, the boat rocked, pitching me forward, and I grabbed the gunwale to steady myself. The sudden movement caused my cell phone to tumble out of my sweatshirt. I watched as it clanged off the side of the boat and fell into the water.

"Great. Just great."

There was nothing I could do about the phone. I went back to the big boat, picked the lock, and opened the cabin door. A bell jangled. I shut the door behind me and found an alarm keypad mounted on the wall next to the door. There was no off switch, only a numerical keypad. I would have to work fast before the police or security arrived.

The interior was a page out of *Better Homes & Gardens*. Light bounced in from the horizontal blinds angled upward but not fully closed. The motif was beige trimmings and black granite, a plush couch and sofa chair on either side of the cabin separated by a throw rug edged in a floral design. Beyond the living area, a granite-top dining table offered seating for four and led towards a well-appointed galley and pantry. At the end of the space was a second door.

I searched the pantry and a closet, even though I knew both areas were too small. The door at the front of the cabin was locked, which I was able to pick in a few seconds. Lacking the windows of the main cabin, the room was pitch dark. I felt along the wall for a switch and flicked on the light to reveal I had found the head.

Piled on the floor, toilet, sink, and vanity were the mailbags. I counted all twenty-four of them stuffed into the space, rising to my chest. I opened one of the bags and pulled out a stack of fifties.

I reached for my phone to call Trujillo and remembered I'd lost the damn thing. The alarm bell continued to clang. After setting several stacks of money atop one of the mail bags, I snapped off three quick shots with my camera.

The original plan was to find the money, call Trujillo, and meet him here. My lost cell phone eliminated that plan. But thinking about it, the alarm would serve the same purpose as a cell phone call. I'd have some explaining to do to the beat cops or the hired security guys, but in the end it would all work out. I also wondered if maybe the alarm just went to a monitoring center, which in turn notified the boat's owner about the intrusion rather than calling the police. I could see the thieves not wanting their stash spotted by snooping cops.

Either way, it made sense for me to remain on the boat. If the cops came, I'd explain the situation and have them summon Trujillo. If they didn't come, and the bad guys did, then I'd use their cell phone to call Sac PD and hold them at gunpoint until they arrived.

I plopped onto the sofa chair, my gun in hand. About five minutes later, the alarm stopped ringing, which I took as a sign a visit from somebody would be imminent.

thirty-seven

WITH MY INDEX FINGER, I eased down a slat in the aluminum blinds to get a view of the parking lot. The parts of the lot I could see remained empty, though much of it was obscured by the business office and a swath of trees.

I sat back down and pondered the implications of what I'd found. People would be going to jail. I went back to the head to take a second look at the bags of money. Just to be sure, I checked the contents of five different bags. It all seemed to be there. Outside on the dock I could hear the loud, swift advance of footsteps. Less than a minute later, the cabin door swung open.

"You should see the look on your face," I said. "I thought 'jaw dropped open' was only an expression. But yours really did."

"What are you…how did you…you have no…" Candace Symingtom was having a hard time finding the right words.

"Take a second, Candace. Collect your thoughts." Aiming my gun at her probably didn't help her composure. "I want you to take off your jacket and toss it over in the corner. Then I want you to turn around so I can see you don't have a weapon stuck in your jeans. Toss your purse over onto the chair." I pointed at the sofa chair with my gun. She did as I asked.

"You made pretty good time," I said. "It's about twenty miles from Rosetown to here. Will the police be joining us?"

She shook her head. "No, the alarm company notified me."

"Too bad. They'd get a kick out of seeing all that money. Sit down on the couch." I kept a close eye on her as I went through her purse, confirming she didn't have a gun hidden inside. I moved back to keep a good six to eight feet between us.

"I can explain," she said.

"I'm sure you can."

"How did you find the money?"

I pointed at her shoes. "Top Siders are boating shoes. And your keys there in your purse. You have a floating keychain. I noticed it the first day we met. People who spend a lot of time in and around boats tend to have those. If you accidentally drop your keys in the water, they'll float so you can retrieve them. It got me to thinking."

She shook her head in disbelief.

"From there it was easy to do an online search about the registered boat owners in California. This one is registered to a Dr. Arthur Symington. Your father, I take it?"

She gave a slight nod.

"I like the name, *Cardinal Rules*. Named after your alma mater, Stanford. Nice of your dad to do that."

She nodded again. She looked sick, her face pale.

"It was a good idea to use a boat to haul away the money. Security here is pretty good. Though, I was able to get in, not to pat myself on the back." I gave her an exaggerated smile. "When were you planning to move the money somewhere else?"

"Eventually."

"It was pretty stupid for you to come barging in here unarmed when you got the call from the alarm company."

"I figured the storm set off the alarm." Her voice was a soft monotone, as if she was still processing the situation. "I'll give you some of the money if you'll go away and drop the whole thing."

"It's funny. When I first started on this assignment, I thought it might be an inside job. You know, someone on Monarch. Then everything hit the fan. Chan gets killed. Forrester and Seeger blow up that damn building. But you went one step too far when you killed Adam Benzer. All of a sudden, the Golden Dragons are in jail. The SCS are in jail. And the only ones left standing are the Monarch project team members. I knew one or more of you had to be behind it all."

"I don't know what you're talking about. I didn't kill anybody."

"It made perfect sense to me," I said, ignoring her. "You were the one who told me on day one that maybe S-SOP stole the project, knowing S-SOP's ties would lead me to the Stone Creek Saviors."

She made no effort to argue the point, looking at me with a mixture of hatred and fear, her dark eyes narrowed and fixed on me.

"Was it just luck the Golden Dragons happened to be in the mix, or did you know Chan and Benzer were into them for a half-million?"

She continued to pierce me with her eyes.

"Then you added the bloody SCS letters at Chan's house. Something was wrong about that. I mean, I could see the Golden Dragons or the SCS as suspects, but not both. Framing them both was overkill. Excuse the pun."

"Are you going to let me talk, or are you going to keep making things up?"

"One more question, and then it's your turn. Are Wiggin and Cassidy both in on it?"

She laughed and shook her head. "You have no idea about anything. No, they had nothing to do with this, nothing at all. They still think SCS got the money."

"You did it all by yourself? The extortion plot? The murders?"

"I didn't kill anybody. Stop saying that!" She looked about the cabin, at the door, the blinds behind me, and then the money.

"How did you hatch this little plan of yours?"

"It was Thomas's idea. I was venting to him one night…about how hard I worked on Monarch…about how little I was going to get out of it." She seemed in shock, her words coming in disjointed bursts, her eyes studying the floor at her feet. "The university…they had all the rights…to the profits…the patents…everything else. They pay me two grand a month…that's it…and I developed something worth several billion dollars. That wasn't fair. Thomas proposed doing something about that."

"He came up with the idea of ransoming it to Sunrise and NAFC?"

"No." Her eyes regained some focus, and she looked at me. "He said he could find a buyer for it in China. He said he could get five or ten million for it. He brought Adam in on it, too."

"What happened to that deal?"

"He didn't have a buyer lined up. They tried shopping it, but they were terrible at explaining the science and technology. They needed me to help them sell it to the technical people at the companies."

"So why didn't you?"

She shrugged. "I was thinking about it, but it would've exposed me. I wasn't sure if one of the Chinese companies might blow the whistle on me. Then Thomas and I broke up as a couple, and I told him I didn't want to do the deal anymore. I was done."

I thought about the first time I saw Thomas Chan outside the Granderson café. He'd stood out there, his palms up, questioning Candace. I'd thought he was playing the jilted lover, but now I realized it was something much more.

"Did you know he was doing business with the Golden Dragons?"

She nodded. "Not by name, but I knew he'd borrowed a lot of money from loan sharks. He was counting on the Monarch deal to get the cash to pay them back. Then that fell through. He was under a lot of pressure to pay them back. Then he kept pushing me to stick to the plan to sell off the project. That's when we broke up. He became this total asshole."

"Benzer was trying to sell Monarch just a couple of days ago. To SMUD."

"He was?" She looked surprised. "Dumb shit. I don't think he knew about what went down already with the project, the ransom and all. He must have panicked because he needed to pay off those thugs and still thought Monarch was in play."

"Do you have a cell phone on you?" I asked. I hadn't noticed one in her purse when I checked it. It was time to call Trujillo and wrap things up.

"No, I was in a hurry. I left it in the car."

She looked again at the cabin door, in the general direction of the parking lot. "I have to use the restroom."

"Good luck with that. It's stuffed with money."

"I'll move it. I need to go bad."

I thought about any downside to her locking herself in with the money. She didn't have a weapon or cell phone in her pockets or anywhere else I could see. The head didn't have a window or other means of escape. I nodded my approval, and she stood and walked to the front of the boat. I turned and watched her as she approached the head when I heard the door behind me open with a bang.

"Drop your gun, asshole!"

I dropped my gun at my feet and turned around. Jerry Langford was aiming a gun at the middle of my chest.

thirty-eight

"JERRY," I SAID, relieved. "I found the money. It was Candace all along."

He smiled. "Candace, pick up his gun and walk over here."

My relief evaporated. Candace grabbed the gun and walked over to Langford, who took it from her and stuck it in the empty holster on his belt. He took a step forward, shutting the cabin door behind him. They stood side by side evaluating me. Langford lowered the gun to his waist, the barrel still trained on me.

"I thought you said it was Thomas Chan's idea," I said to Candace.

"It was," Langford said, answering for her. "But then I saw an opportunity and a way to sweeten the deal for Ms. Symington here."

"I'm not following."

"When we first met, you said something to the effect you were surprised I didn't know what was going on in Wiggin's lab. I had to bite my tongue not to tell you I knew everything. About Monarch. About Candace and Thomas. And I know everything else that happens on campus."

"You knew about Monarch? You and Candace orchestrated the theft and the extortion?"

"Of course. I saw Candace and Chan on camera one evening arguing in a Sieboldt lab. Most people don't know it, but I've also got audio monitoring in most of the classrooms and labs. At first I thought it was a lovers' quarrel, but after a minute or two of listening it was obvious they'd been planning to steal Wiggin's research project and sell it overseas. Candace was frustrated Chan couldn't sell the project and kept dropping the price to potential buyers. They broke up then and there, and any plan involving Monarch was over. That's when I contacted Candace with a sweeter deal than her ex-boyfriend could ever offer. Under my plan, she could have her cake and eat it, too."

"You got twenty million dollars and the safe return of the project," I said.

Candace would not meet my eyes.

"Ten million apiece," Langford said. "Not a bad pension, considering the shitty salary and lack of respect Granderson shows me."

Candace looked uncomfortable standing next to Langford. I couldn't tell if it was what he was saying or if she just didn't like him.

"What are you going to do to me?" I already knew the answer but wanted him to say it.

"Candace is quite the skilled boatsman, excuse me, boatswoman. You should have seen her navigate this thing onto the beach. Fifteen minutes later we were back on our way here. Mission accomplished. You'll see for yourself in a minute; she's going to take us for a little cruise." He glanced at her.

Candace seemed a little surprised at the news we would be going somewhere in her dad's boat. "Can't we just pay him to go away? I'll give it to him out of my cut."

"Don't be naive, Candace. Even if we gave him some money, even if he took it, he's not going to let this go. Am I right, Ray?"

I thought about playing with him and saying I'd take hush money, but I knew he'd see through it. There was no point in doing that little dance with him. I did want to delay our departure as long as I could while I scoured my brain for something—anything—to get me out of this mess.

"Why did you hire me to look into the theft of Monarch when you didn't really want the truth to be known?"

He laughed.

"Did you think I couldn't figure it out?" I asked.

"Nothing personal. I didn't think anyone would figure it out. I had to make it look like I took the whole business seriously. I didn't want to bring in the police. I thought about handling the investigation myself, but it would look more credible by hiring an independent contractor. Besides, you made a terrific bagman."

"Hell of an act you put on on my porch the other day," I said. "Pretending to be pissed off because of the twenty million and not keeping you in the loop. You convinced me." I wanted to stroke his considerable ego in hopes he might let down his guard. They both stood more than ten feet away. I stood in the small galley and looked for something I might be able to throw at him. There was a wood-block with five or six knives in it well beyond my reach. The only objects I might be able to grab were wooden salt and pepper shakers.

Langford smiled smugly. "I thought the follow-up phone call after you'd been on campus was a nice touch, too. 'What part of not setting foot on campus do you not understand?'" he said in an exaggerated voice, repeating the line he'd given me the other day on the phone. He laughed.

"And how did you set up the whole thing with Forrester?"

"I told you I know everything going on at Granderson, including that crazy fuck Forrester. I knew he and Seth Seeger, the little prick, were up to something. I didn't know what because they used these little code words. Thought they were clever. Anyway, I wanted to keep you busy and take your eye off the ball so to speak. So I made it look like SCS was behind the extortion. They were perfect for my misdirec-tion." Langford relished telling me the details of his plan, wanting me to marvel at his brilliance.

"I was telling Candace implicating SCS and the Golden Dragons worked against you. It didn't make sense they would both be involved in Chan's and Benzer's murders. It helped me put it together."

He bristled at the suggestion he'd made anything approaching a mistake or a misstep. "The Dragons cut the fingers off of Chan on their own. I had nothing to do with that. It helped my cause. My plan all along was to make it look like SCS was behind it. The Dragon angle complicated things, which was good. It kept you and the police looking in the wrong direction."

"And you killed both Chan and Benzer?"

He nodded.

Candace turned and looked at him. "Wait a minute. *You* killed Thomas? I thought the Dragons—"

"Had to be done. He wasn't going to back off hounding you for Monarch so he could pay off the Dragons. He would have wrecked the whole thing."

She looked a mix of surprise, disbelief, and anger. Her breathing deepened and quickened. She looked like she might hyperventilate, her eyes glassing over, turning inward in thought.

"I like the way you staged Chan's death, by the way," I said. "Stabbed on his bed, like maybe he knew the killer, like maybe they were intimate. Sure, you had the SCS written on the wall. And the Golden Dragons were in the mix. But if the cops ruled them out for any reason, the next suspect might have been a woman. Maybe a recent girlfriend." I looked at Candace to see if my words were stoking her anger. "Benzer you just shot. No need to stage anything. You had the money. You were home free. He was a loose end because he knew about the original plan to steal the project. If he found out about the ransom payout, who knows what he might have done. You couldn't risk having him around."

Langford nodded.

"You killed Adam, too? You son of a bitch! I didn't get into this to kill anybody. I just wanted what I was due."

"Not only that, Candace," I said. "But after he's done killing me and dumping my body into the river miles from here, my guess is you're next. Twenty million is a lot more satisfying than ten."

"You bastard!" she screamed, slapping him hard on the face.

Stunned, Langford turned to look at her. "Candace, it's not like that. I—"

She slapped him again, harder even than the first blow, turning his face and body to one side. I bolted towards him as fast and as low to the ground as I could. He saw me when I was two steps away, and he fired his gun, his aim just over my head. My shoulder drove into his solar plexus, and he groaned as we fell against the cabin door, which sprang open on the impact, sending us sprawling onto the narrow back ledge of the boat.

I had the advantage since I was on top of him, and I wrested the gun from his grip. It slipped from my hand and cartwheeled in the air. I heard it splash in the river. He heaved and jerked so violently I knew I couldn't hold him much longer. If he broke free, he'd be able to reach for my gun in his holster. Releasing my grip on his left wrist, I brought my cupped hand above my shoulder and walloped him as hard as I could on his left ear. He howled with pain. I reached down to his belt and grabbed my gun, rolling off him.

I scrambled to my feet and pointed the gun at him as he rolled over and tried to stand.

"Stay down," I commanded.

He started to stand again, and I fired. The shot shattered the fiberglass six inches from his right foot. Langford went down to his knees in surrender. Candace stood, slack-jawed, a couple of feet away inside the cabin.

"This thing has a radio, doesn't it?" I asked.

She nodded, a hand covering her mouth, eyes wide, tears streaming down her face.

"Use it to call the police. Ask for a Lieutenant Trujillo."

epilogue

WE CRUISED UP HOWE AVENUE, unsure of what to say to each other. We'd not said a word since we both entered the new Lexus ES 350, and I drove it off the lot. Danny Cashmore called me back after three weeks. Our telephone conversation had been brief. He asked if I could meet him at the dealership, and we picked a time. When I knocked on his office door, he stood, tossed me the car keys, and said we were going for a drive.

"You got my messages?" I asked.

"Yeah, why do you think I called you? You're a long-winded bastard, I have to say. Damn near filled up my voice mail box."

We drove in silence for a few more minutes. The car handled beautifully, and I could get used to the all-leather interior and how quiet it was inside, even as we drove down one of Sacramento's busiest streets.

"Some of the standard interior features include a compass and tach. It's got a memory moon roof and automatic temperature control. Eight speakers. You can get an integrated navigation system and heated steering wheel for a few extra bucks."

"Does it have a blind-spot warning?"

"Check it out." Danny pointed to the passenger side mirror. On cue, a car moved into my blind spot on my right, and a red light in the mirror started to blink.

We hit a red light at Hurley, and I eased the car to a stop. "I like it."

"You know, Jolene and I split up."

"I didn't know. I'm sorry."

"I'm not mad at you, Ray. I overreacted. Once Jolene calmed down a week or so later, we had a good conversation. In the end, she just didn't think I was the right guy for her. And maybe she's right. I am still a little immature for my age. I admit it."

"You? Nah?" And I couldn't help but laugh. "Impulsive maybe. Immature? I don't think so."

"Anyway, she told me what happened with you two. You didn't hit on her. So, I'm sorry I got ticked off at you."

"You don't need to apologize. I handled the whole thing badly. Should never have—"

He stopped me with a wave of his hand. "Just so you know, if you want to ask her out, I'd be okay with it."

"No." I shook my head. "Besides, I doubt she would answer the phone if I called."

"No, she would. She likes you. And you're both really good people. Go for it."

"I don't think it's a good idea."

The light turned green, and we continued up Howe towards the interstate. I looked over my right shoulder, signaled, and moved the car from the left lane to the middle.

"I read about your work at Granderson. If I'd known you were neck deep in all that shit, I wouldn't have bothered you about looking into Jolene. The college chick and the security chief stealing twenty million bucks and killing those two guys."

"Yeah, it was something."

"When does the trial start?"

"Not for a while. They've got conspiracy charges, extortion, grand theft, and on top of it all, murder. Candace deserves everything but the murder rap, but I guess that's what she gets for playing with fire."

"Is their project as great as they said on the news? They made it sound like it was the biggest thing since the Internet."

"We'll see. The investors think so. And so does the professor leading it." Turned out Wiggin did have a sister on Delta Queen Avenue. I never made the effort to see if he was housesitting there the night of the drop, but I assumed he was. I left him a voice mail apology but never heard back from him.

"Pretty nice ride, don't you think?" Danny asked. "I'd be glad to sell you this one, or one like it, for my cost."

"I don't want you to lose money on the deal," I said.

Danny laughed. "You shouldn't believe half the stuff any car dealer says, especially me. I'm still making money selling the car at cost."

I gave him a quizzical look.

"Don't ask," he said.

We reached the onramp to westbound I-80. I made a left turn and hit the accelerator to see how the car would respond.

"Lots of giddyup, huh?"

"Yeah," I agreed.

"Were you really there when those greenie terrorists blew up the Voncabo building in Woodland?"

"Yeah, I got there too late. They go to trial in six months. Between them, Langford and Symington, I'll be spending half of the next year or so in depositions and testifying in court." I pulled into the fast lane and eased my speed up to seventy-five. "And I almost forgot about Wu and Bo—the two Golden Dragons. They moved them down to LA for trial. But if they ever try them in Sacramento for assaulting Benzer, I'll have to testify in that case, too."

We continued down the freeway without talking for several minutes. Danny took a call from one of his salesmen and approved a deal on a GS 460. He then called his finance manager to tell him about the price he'd approved so he'd be ready with the paperwork.

"You seeing anybody new yet, Danny?"

He smiled. "Yeah, you know me. I've got to have something on the line all the time or I go crazy. The assistant golf pro at the club. Thirty-five years old. Tight little—"

"Okay," I said. "I don't want any more information. And I'm not going to check this one out for you."

"I wasn't going to ask," he said, and we both laughed.

The End

Did you like this book? If so, please take a minute to rate it on Amazon. Ratings really help authors like me.

Get a FREE Copy of *Courage Begins*

Read the prequel to *Courage Matters*

(Go to http://www.rscottmackey.com/?page_id=163
for **free** download page)

In this prequel to *Courage Matters*, Ray Courage begins his private investigation career, displaying the skills, abilities and sense of humor that have made him a fan favorite around the world.

About the Author

Scott Mackey lives in Northern California, where he writes both fiction and non-fiction His Ray Courage Mystery books have received international acclaim.

Follow him:

Twitter: smackey17

Facebook: Facebook.com/rscottmackey

Goodreads: http://bit.ly/1tMtfF8

Web: www.rscottmackey.com

More Ray Courage...

Available now on Amazon and other online retailers

Courage Begins: A Ray Courage Novella
Former college professor Ray Courage starts a new career as a private investigator and tries to crack an unsolved murder. In this prequel to *Courage Matters*, Ray Courage begins his private investigation career, displaying the skills, abilities and sense of humor that have made him a fan favorite around the world.

Courage Matters
Rookie Private Investigator Ray Courage is asked by "Stockbroker to the Stars" Lionel Stroud to investigate an employee who's been acting suspiciously. Ray soon learns that not everything is as it appears at Stroud's firm. When his investigation uncovers a possible Ponzi Scheme orchestrated by Stroud himself, two people are murdered and Ray becomes Suspect Number One. Ray needs to find answers fast to avoid prison… or death at the hands of the killer.

Courage Resurrected
Ray Courage's wife Pam died thirteen years before in a car accident. Or did she? Ray receives e-mails from someone claiming to be his dead wife, accusing him of attempting to kill her and vowing revenge. As he deals with the possibility that his wife is still alive, he tries to find who's behind the threatening messages. As he does, Ray must outrun the police and elude a murderous predator.

Acknowledgements

First of all I would like to thank my editor from Indie Books Gone Wild, Jennifer Oberth, who is an absolute joy to work with. Her editorial skills have vastly improved this manuscript by finding errors, omissions, incongruities, inconsistencies and so on. If there are any mistakes left in this book the fault is all mine. I would also like to thank Indie Books Gone Wild proofreader Karen Robinson, whose work notched up the quality of this book even more. Thank you both for the great work you do.

And again, I can't thank Karen Phillips enough for the great cover designs she comes up with time and again. This is her fourth cover in the Ray Courage Series. It is her work and creativity that have helped create the Ray Courage "brand," making it stand out in crowded e-bookshelves. I look forward to working with her on the next book in the series.

www.ingramcontent.com/pod-product-compliance
Lightning Source LLC
Chambersburg PA
CBHW021035130626
46552CB00005B/1855